Lies We Tell
Secrets We Keep

Pamela Harris Williams

www.inspiteofpublications.com

Also By Pamela Harris Williams

Take Another Look: See Yourself the Way God
Sees You

This is a work of fiction. All of the characters, organizations, and events portrayed in this novel are either products of the author's imagination or are used fictitiously.

www.inspiteofpublications.com

ISBN-13: 978-0615774039
ISBN-10: 0615774032
First Edition: March 2013

Editors: Pamela Harris Williams, Geneva Currie, Vivian Jones, Katrina Sweet
Interior Design: Pamela Harris Williams
Cover Design: Lance Varner of Game Changers

Dedication

Lies We Tell Secrets We Keep is dedicated to my very best friends of more than twenty-five years-Felicia Berry, Cherry Walker, Romie Holmes, and Patches. It is because of our barrier-breaking, storm-withstanding friendship that I was inspired and this book was written. Thank you for the many wonderful years we've shared together, and the awesome years still to come.

Acknowledgments

I would like to thank several people for helping to make this book possible. Thanks to the two loves of my life, my children- Avery and Malik. Thank you for being proud of me when I found it hard to be proud of myself. I love you two sweeties to life!

Thanks to my momma, Johnnie Mae Harris, for always being there with the "kick in the behind" I needed. I love you more than you can fathom.

Thanks to a few special people- Vivian Jones, Katrina Sweet, Geneva Currie, Theresa White, Beatrice Fields, Shateeka Jones, and Queen Johnson- Thanks for holding my hand when I needed it, for shaking me back to reality when I needed it, and for giving of yourselves selflessly to assist me with this project.

I would also like to thank Lance Varner, of Game Changers, for creating an awesome book cover. You did good son! LOL

Last but not least, I want to thank God for strengthening me to endure the changes and processes in life (even when I created a mess) so I could share His life, and ultimately His death, with so many more deserving people.

~1~
"Could It Get Any Worse?"

"Richard, aren't you getting up," I asked as I sped pass our bed headed for the bathroom. He was always oversleeping and this was the second time this week I was running late for work. I surely didn't want to hear my supervisor's mouth about punctuality again this morning. You see it was my husband's fault why "late" had become my middle name. Richard's the type of guy who waits until the very last minute to get ready and doesn't plan for any mishaps or accidents. Obviously this morning was going to be a repeat of Monday. Richard hadn't responded, so I stopped putting on mascara long enough to peep my head into the bedroom to see if he had heard me. "Richard, did you hear me," I asked as I slowly approached the bed. "Your toast and eggs are ready downstairs. Get up babe, or we'll both be late for work... again!" Still, there was no response. He must've really been tired from our date on last night, I thought to myself as I smiled while reminiscing over the events from the prior evening.

I sat slowly on the edge of the bed behind him and gently began to massage his shoulder with hopes it would wake him, but I realized he hadn't shifted positions at all. "Our date on last night must've really worn him out," I whispered to myself while beaming with a smile from ear to ear. I gently reached over and touched his shoulder again to wake him and, "Oh my God! Richard! Richard!" I screamed frantically as I ran and grabbed the phone to dial 9-1-1. Somehow, in between sobbing uncontrollably and not being able to catch my breath, I managed to relay my address to the operator. All I remember from that moment on was slowly sliding down the wall until my bottom rested on the floor and crying so hysterically that my body convulsed. I was frantic, scared, and confused. Richard was not only my husband of seventeen years, but he was my very best friend. What would I do without him?

Everything from that point on is a complete blur. Somehow, my neighbor managed to contact why he didn't respond when I called him. So I went over to try and wake him and that's when...." I couldn't bring myself to utter another word about what took place earlier this morning. "It's going to be okay Liz," Tangie spoke softly as she hugged me and rocked me in her arms as I cried.

Tangie and I sat there for what seemed like hours waiting for the doctor to come in and talk to us concerning Richard. I don't know what I would've done if Tangie wasn't here with me. She told me she'd phoned Cat and Celeste, our other two girlfriends, and told them what had happened. They were both making preparations to come and be with me during this time. I can't remember the last time we were all together. This gathering wasn't exactly how I would've planned for us to see one another again though. Out of the four of us, Tangie and I were the closest. We'd all grown up in Cary, North Carolina just outside of Charlotte where we attended school together. School, however, wasn't where we became close friends though. No, we actually became friends through the Sunday school class we were all attended with our teacher, Mrs. Goodwin.

In our little circle of friends, there's Tangie-the head strong, rational, yet nurturing one. She was like the "mother" of the group, and we all knew better than to cross her because if you did-there would be hell to pay. There's Celeste-the very attractive and overly confident one. None of us would ever admit it, but we were all a little jealous of her because, even at the age of nine, Celeste was voluptuous and well developed. While we were all stuffing our bras with tissue to look shapely like Celeste, she was already developed enough to wear her mother's bras. When we were younger, all the boys gravitated towards her and the men still do till this day and she absolutely enjoys the attention. Then there is Cat, short for Catherine. She was always very observant, very shy, and very cautious. Cat is that girlfriend in the group who would always ask, "What if we get caught." She was always the voice of reason- you know that overly cautious person in the group who constantly wondered what momma would say. All of my girlfriends were coming to be with me during this horrible and lonely time and I needed and wanted them here more than anything. "Tangie, I can't think of any other people I would want to be with at this time than the three of you guys, especially since mom and dad aren't here anymore."

Shortly thereafter, the doctor came in to inform me of what he believed had happened to Richard. "Mrs. Frazier," the doctor whispered as he extended his hand to greet me. "Hi, I'm Dr. Fitzpatrick. Can I talk with you in the family room," he asked as he motioned towards the room. Tangie and I stood and walked towards the waiting room just around the corner from where we were sitting. After closing the door behind us, Dr. Fitzpatrick slowly took a seat and commenced giving me his version of what he thought had happened to my husband. "Mrs. Frazier, have you ever heard of Congenital Abnormalities of the Heart," he asked. I looked at him confused, "No I haven't. Why? My husband didn't have any heart problems." "Well Mrs. Frazier, just from what I've found thus far, your husband had an overgrown ventricular muscle," he said as he slid a photo in front of me to look at. "I would venture to say your husband was probably born this way." "How is this possible? Richard never complained of any chest pains. He was in great shape. He ran three times a week and he was very particular about what he ate." "Mrs. Frazier, most people who suffer with this abnormality aren't aware they even have it and the symptoms are often confused with those of heartburn or acid reflux. This type of defect often causes ventricular fibrillation, or an irregular heartbeat. Mrs. Frazier, during ventricular fibrillation, numerous electrical discharges are sent to the chamber of the heart resulting in blood no longer being pumped." As I sat there listening to the doctor, my mind wandered back to the date my husband and I had just on last night. It was like we were on our first date again. Richard didn't speak much, but he said so much in his actions. There was this mysterious, yet intriguing charm about him, which I attributed to his quietness. He wasn't a man of many words, but he said so much with his eyes and his actions. After our dinner and movie date, we went home where we cuddled on the couch in front of the fireplace. We said nothing as we watched the flames dancing in front of us. Even in our silence, so much more was being said and we knew exactly what the other was speaking. We were finally content and happy with it just being the two of us, but at one point in our lives we both wanted children. We were unable to have any though. After having received this devastating news, Richard did everything in his power to ensure I was happy- even going as far as surprising me with handwritten letters and love notes when he knew things were bothering me. I will never forget those words he wrote to me when we found out we couldn't have children, "Lizzy, I love you just the way you are. No additions to our family or lack thereof will ever change how much I love and care for you. If you remember nothing else I say, please know that I AM ABSOLUTELY IN LOVE WITH YOU and not with what you can or cannot give me. I will love you regardless." Those words took my breath away. As I thought back, I began to tear up again and both Tangie and Dr. Fitzpatrick stopped and looked at me. "Liz, do you want the doctor to stop," Tangie asked as she leaned in closer towards me. "I was just remembering something Richard told me," I said as I placed my hands over my face and began to cry. "Mrs. Frazier, I can see how terribly upset you are and I will respect that. I'll put all of my findings in a report and ensure you receive a copy of it. If there is anything else I can do to help make this process a little more bearable, please let me know. Again, my condolences," he whispered as he stood and turned to leave the room. Eventually Dr. Fitzpatrick's nurse came in and gave me the coroner's information, but before she left the room, she handed me a small plastic bag. "Mrs. Frazier, here are your husband's personal belongings," she said as she gently placed the small bag in my hand. "If there is anything- absolutely anything, I can do, please don't hesitate in asking. The coroner's office is awaiting your phone call to discuss arrangements. And again, I am so sorry for your loss Mrs. Frazier," she said as she turned and exited the room. As I slowly opened the bag, my stomach began to churn again. I gently reached in to remove the small object from the bottom of the bag. It was Richard's wedding band! My eyes filled with tears as I slid his ring on my thumb and gently kissed it. As badly as I wanted this all to be over or to be able to rewind the last twenty-four hours of my life, I somehow knew I had yet to experience the magnitude of sadness and loneliness that awaited me. I knew things would become far worse for me before getting any better.

The next morning I awoke in our bed and, out of habit, I reached over to feel for Richard, but he wasn't there. My mind quickly began playing tricks on me. "Maybe he's downstairs making me breakfast. I know- I'll act surprised when he comes into the room," I whispered to myself as I tried to look as though I was asleep. I suddenly started smelling the aroma of freshly brewed coffee and that alone further proved Richard was indeed downstairs pouring me a cup of my favorite- hazelnut coffee. I had somehow convinced myself last night was a horrible dream and, at any moment, I would hear Richard's footsteps climbing the stairs to kiss me good morning before handing me my coffee. No sooner than the thought crossed my mind, did I hear footsteps climbing the stairs. I quickly adjusted my head on the pillow and closed my eyes, trying my hardest not to smile. The door slowly opened, and.... "Liz, are you up," Tangie asked as she peeped her head in. She entered slowly revealing my coffee mug. The harsh reality of yesterday's events came crashing down on me the moment I heard Tangie's voice. Everything within me wanted those footsteps to belong to Richard, but they didn't. I then remembered Tangie stayed with me on last night. "I thought you could use a warm cup of coffee this morning. Three creamers and one sugar, right," she said as she gently sat on the edge of the bed and handed me my mug. "You remembered how I liked my coffee? Thanks Tangie. Do you have a Valium to go along with this coffee," I asked with a smirk on my face. "I sat and watched you until you fell asleep last night. You tossed and turned for what seemed like hours and finally you fell asleep," Tangie whispered as she began to straighten the covers on the bed attempting to avoid any direct eye contact. "Yeah, I kept dreaming about Richard." I did my absolute best to appear strong and in control in front of Tangie, but the reality of it was I was broken, hurt, and so very lonely.

"I spoke with Celeste and Cat this morning. Both their planes should arrive later this evening,"

Tangie mentioned as she headed to the bathroom to draw me a bath. "So, what are our plans this morning," she asked as she peeped her head back into the bedroom. "I have to contact the coroner's office and the funeral home," I whispered as I twirled Richard's wedding band around my thumb. That's exactly where it remained after the nurse had given it to me on last night. God how I missed that man! Even with Tangie here, I still felt so very lonely. "Well whatever you have to do, you don't have to do it alone. That's what girlfriends are for," Tangie said as she smiled and proceeded to finish running my bath water. I sat there reminiscing on all the plans Richard and I made. We were looking forward to growing old together. There were lots and lots of things I took for granted while Richard was alive and I wish I could redeem the time. After bathing, Tangie practically had to force feed me breakfast. I had absolutely no appetite- eating was the farthest thing from my mind. Shortly thereafter, we were out the door and headed to the coroner's office. I wanted, more than anything, for this nightmare to be over. Widowed at thirty-seven- I never imagined it would happen to me.

Richard was never coming back and the loneliness I felt only heightened because there was no one left on the face of the earth to remind me of him. His adoptive parents were dead, and Richard had never known his biological family. His adoptive parents never had any children, and they never adopted any other children outside of Richard. So Richard and I were the last of our immediate families. Now that Richard was gone, I was left here all alone to fend for myself- a very sad and lonely widow.

~2~
"A Unified Front"

"Tangie, did you hear the doorbell," I asked as I made my way to the stairs. "Yeah, I got it. It's Celeste," she yelled as she opened the door slowly. As soon as I reached the bottom of the stairs, Celeste dropped her bags and bolted towards me with tears in her eyes. "Hey Liz," she said as she gently embraced me. "Hey Celeste, it's good to see you," I whispered as I slowly headed for the living room. I was amazed at how mentally and physically exhausted I was and it was obviously evident in my body language and voice. "Liz you sound tired baby. Are you getting any rest," Celeste asked as she tucked a pillow behind my head for me to rest on. "Well Celeste, I've been getting as much rest as I possibly can," I whispered while managing to squeeze a smile out from amongst all the hurt and inner turmoil overwhelming me. I couldn't help but notice how much makeup Celeste was wearing though. She looked like she was trying to cover up

19

something.   Not to mention the clothes she wore were a little warm for the weather we were having here in Charlotte. The temperature was around 75 degrees and Celeste was wearing a wool pullover sweater and thick leggings with knee high boots. Maybe the weather in DC, where she had come from, was a little cooler. Yeah that was it or so I tried to convince myself. No matter how hard I tried to silence the scenarios my mind yelled at me concerning Celeste and how she looked, I absolutely couldn't. It was obvious she was dealing with something. What baffled me more than anything was how it was even possible for Celeste to endure so much, and her very best friends weren't even aware of it. Some friends we were, I thought to myself while trying my best not to stare at her. Celeste was definitely dealing with or possibly even hiding something and hopefully by the end of our time together, I would know exactly what or who it was.

"So Tangie, how's life with you," Celeste asked sarcastically as she shifted in her chair to face Tangie. It was obvious she had only said that to make small talk and she really didn't care how Tangie's life was going. The tension between the two of them hadn't just become this way- no it started in the ninth grade. I'll never forget the evening of our freshman dance. Tangie had gone with Brandon Carter, one of the boys from the neighborhood who lived three houses down from mine. As far back as I can remember, Brandon had always tried to sleep with Tangie, but she consistently refused. He was determined to change her mind though. Brandon had tried, on several occasions, to get Tangie off by herself- away from the rest of us, but Tangie wasn't having it though. Despite Tangie's repeated refusals, she really liked Brandon and we all knew it. Later that night after the dance, Brandon walked Tangie home and they kissed for the very first time. Of course he tried to take it further, but Tangie pushed him away. She later told me she really wanted to do it, but she kept hearing Mrs. Goodwin's voice in her head, "Young ladies remember you can always be one of those girls who's having sex, but they can never be a virgin like you ever again no matter how hard they try. You have the upper hand here, so use it." After Tangie and I finished our phone call that night, I'd heard a female's voice outside- so I stepped on the front porch to see who it was. It was Celeste! What was she doing at Brandon's house?

We later found out Celeste was indeed interested in Brandon and she had even gone as far as sleeping with him. Why would she do something so scandalous? She knew, heck we all knew how much Tangie really liked him. Of course that was the first, but it would not be the last time we experienced Celeste's backstabbing ways. People constantly asked us why we didn't cut her lose after she messed around with Brandon. The average person would not have put up with her, but they didn't know what she endured a few years prior. It wasn't until after that horrible summer night, that Celeste changed for the worse. We never talked about that night after it happened, partly because we didn't want to dredge up the horrible memories. When we were twelve and thirteen years old, we were on our way home from a long hot, but fun day at the community pool. We'd been swimming all day and now the sun had started to set and we were in a hurry to get back to Tangie's house where we would all be staying over for a slumber party. We were only about three blocks away from Tangie's house when three men jumped out from behind the bushes and started pulling on our bathing suits and teasing us. We told them to stop and to leave us alone, but they wouldn't. Tangie and Cat managed to break free and run towards the house, but Celeste and I weren't so lucky. They managed to drag me and Celeste into the woods, kicking and screaming. No one heard us and no one came to help us. What was taking Cat and Tangie so long to send help? Somehow I bit the arm of the man holding me and managed to break free and I started to run, but I turned back because I couldn't leave Celeste. All I remember was the fearful and tearful look in her eyes as she yelled, "Run Liz! Go get help! Hurry Liz, hurry," as they took her farther into the woods. Everything in me wanted to go into those woods and get my friend, but I knew I would be no match for those guys. So I ran for help as hard and as fast as I could. As I was running, I could hear her screaming, "Help me! Help me!" Why couldn't anyone else hear her screaming? My God, what were they doing to her? Before I could reach the house, Tangie's dad and her brothers met me with sticks in their hands. "Liz, where's Celeste," her dad asked as he approached me. "She's down there in the woods," I whispered obviously out of breath, as I pointed down the street. "Three guys took her. Help her please," I said as I fell to my knees out of breath and in tears. When Tangie's dad found Celeste, she was lying in fetal position crying. He gently lifted her in his arms and carried her back to the house where he phoned the police and her mother. Tangie's brother's faces said it all. I don't believe what they witnessed that night was something they could've ever imagined happening to someone so near and dear to their family. Tangie, Cat, and I all sat on the couch huddled together crying hysterically and frantically. I'll never forget the look on Celeste's face. It was the very look I'd seen on the faces of the female victims on those Lifetime movies mom had forbidden me to watch, but I managed to watch anyway when she wasn't home. I later came to realize that look was the very face of shame and embarrassment. The once free and liberated girl I knew was no more.

Celeste's life, from that very moment, was never the same again. It had suddenly taken a turn for the worse and as time went on she became more and more promiscuous or as the older women put it, "fast." Not long after the attack, she started messing around with Brandon, Tangie's boyfriend. Celeste acted as if she was afraid of being alone. There were always men in her company at any given time. I felt horrible for her after the attack because she carried the guilt, condemnation, and embarrassment on her like a straight jacket she couldn't break free from. They never found the guys who attacked her, and secretly I didn't want them to. I was carrying my very own secret no one knew about and it all stemmed from the night of the attack.

Celeste dated lots and lots of guys in the years to follow. She was never really serious about any of them nor did she have any real or lasting relationships with any of them either. She was in search of something- possibly love or some exaggerated, unrealistic form of security. Each time we were together as a group, she had a different guy with her. Before we had a chance to become familiar with any of them, she'd discard them like the weekly garbage and meet someone new the very next day. Come to think of it, there was this one guy she referred to often- but none of us knew who he was nor had we ever met him. She never mentioned his name, but only referred to him as her "boo." He was the one constant thing in her life, but all the secrecy made me think he meant her no good and she knew we'd disagree with the relationship. Who was this mystery man and what was Celeste hiding?

Before long, the doorbell rang. It had to be Cat because everyone else had already arrived. Sure enough, as Tangie opened the door, there stood the very poised and petite Cat. She was always the smallest of the group, but she possessed the biggest and brightest smile of us all- a smile that would light up any dreary room. "Hey girls," she yelled as she entered the front door with both hands weighed down with luggage. Tangie gave her a hug and a kiss, but Celeste didn't budge from her chair. "Hey

Cat," Celeste said as she waved at her from her seat. Celeste didn't even turn around to look at her. What was that all about? "Well hey to you to Celeste," Cat said as she smiled and headed towards the couch where I was resting. She knelt down in front of the couch and kissed me on my forehead. "Hey Liz. How's my girl holding up," she asked as she pushed my legs back further so she could sit near me on the couch. "I'm okay Cat. How are you and those beautiful children," I asked as I sat up to get a better view of her. I always thought she was the prettiest of all of us. She always had a feminine way about her, very dainty and delicate- the way I always pictured a woman should be. "I'm fine and you know those kids are growing like weeds," she said as she searched her purse for pictures. "I got some pictures somewhere," she said as she rambled through her bag. "I can see them later. Let's get you settled in first and then we can look at pictures," I said as I stood to show her where she would be sleeping. Those kids were her life. If it wasn't for the wedding band on her finger, no one would know she was married because she hardly ever talked about her husband, Chris.

That night we all sat around the kitchen table making small talk and preparing for what was to come from this gathering. We had no clue our lives were about to be turned upside down during this unfortunate reunion. We would never be the same again after this visit as we would all experience things, both individually and collectively, that would rock the very core of our being and cause us to face things we thought we had long since overcome. This was not just a gathering to celebrate the life of my husband Richard, but it would soon turn out to be the meeting grounds for the resurrection of some very painful times in each of our lives. We all had to face these painful times in order to successfully move on with our lives. It soon became obvious we hadn't triumphed over our misfortunes individually, but now that we were all together again- maybe we could successfully overcome those misfortunes collectively as a group of unified girlfriends.

~3~
"All Up in My Business"

"Look Chris, I'm not arguing with you about this right now," Cat whispered in the phone as I walked into the kitchen. She did her best to keep her conversation with her husband private, but that was virtually impossible with her unpredictable episodes of angry outbursts. "Yeah, let me call you back in a few," she said as she rushed off the phone. "Everything alright Cat," I asked glancing at her while pouring myself a cup of juice. "Yeah, girl everything is fine", she stated as she smiled and rested her hand on my shoulder trying to further convince me that she was fine. "I was just reminding Chris to take Sarah to get some tights for her recital on Wednesday, that's all." It was obvious she didn't want me in her business, but I decided to meddle further. "Okay, but you seemed a little upset when I walked into the kitchen," I mentioned concerned. "Nothing I can't handle Liz, but thanks for your concern," she said brushing me off as she left the kitchen. Something was going on with her she wasn't telling us about. When Cat and I talked on the phone, rarely was Chris ever home. I remember asking her on several occasions, "Girl, where's Chris. It's awfully quiet in there. I know those kids are asleep; it's a wonder he isn't in there trying to take your night gown off." She would laugh and respond, "Girl, he's hanging out with the fellas tonight." He was always with the fellas. Truthfully, I was never really fond of Chris in the beginning. I'll never forget when Cat was in labor with CJ, he never made it to the hospital for the birth of his son. His excuse was, "Cat, I got caught up in traffic." Time and time again, Cat would excuse him and the blatantly obvious lies he would tell her. Personally, I always thought there was another woman, but I wouldn't dare voice that to Cat.

Cat was always the fragile one in the group. She wasn't only fragile physically because of her small and petite frame, but she was also fragile emotionally. Her feelings were very easily hurt. When we were little girls, my momma would always say, "That girl wears her heart on her sleeve." As a child, I never knew what she meant by that cliché. Later I realized Cat's feelings were like egg shells and we had to tread softly, as to not crush or hurt them. I wanted to ask her if she thought Chris was seeing another woman, but somehow I already knew what her answer would be. Cat and Chris were married three years after Richard and I and they seemed extremely happy during the first two years of their marriage. Not long thereafter though, Cat began to show signs of worry and stress.

"Cat, is there anything you want to talk about," I asked as I sat down next to her on the couch being careful not to spill my juice in my lap. Now was the perfect time to have this conversation with her because Tangie had already gone to bed and some random guy had stopped by earlier to pick Celeste up and she hadn't come back yet. "Why do you ask Liz? I told you everything was okay," she said obviously a little aggravated at my continuous arsenal of questions. "I know you did, but I wasn't totally convinced though," I said as I turned to face her. She sad nothing, so I began sharing with her some of the things Richard and I endured early on in our marriage. I wanted her to understand even those marriages that looked perfect from the outside were in fact far from such. "Do you remember when I came to stay with you that one time and you asked why Richard hadn't come with me?" "Yeah, what about it," she whispered inquisitively. "Well, during that time I had considered leaving Richard." "What! Why? You two had just gotten married. What could've possibly been wrong with your marriage? The two of you, no doubt, were made for each other. What happened," she asked curiously. "Well, that was around the time I found out I couldn't have children. I didn't tell you, but I was a little jealous when you told me you were pregnant. I wanted so badly to be able to give Richard a child, but no matter how hard we tried- it never happened. So I thought his life would be better off and less painful if I wasn't in it." As those words rolled off my lips, I realized for the first time how stupid they sounded. How would leaving Richard cause him less pain? "Did you ever wonder why I couldn't have children," I asked as I picked at my fingernails. Picking at my nails was a sign I had become uncomfortable and nervous. I did it to draw the attention away from my face where all my emotions were. "We all wondered, but I figured it was too painful to talk about, so I didn't press the issue," Cat said as she turned in her seat. "Why can't you have kids Liz," she asked. By this time, I was cringing in my seat because I regretted even bringing up the subject of children in the first place. My infertility was a very sensitive and painful topic that I'd chosen to remain silent about. I never even shared why I couldn't have kids with my husband nor did I share it with any of my best friends. Talking about my infertility meant I'd have to relive that painful time of my life all over again, and by no means did I plan on doing that not now, not ever. "It's getting a little late Cat, and you know I have to be at the funeral home at 9 AM. Get some rest and we'll talk about it on tomorrow," I said knowing I would never bring this conversation up ever again. "Okay Liz, if you say so. You get some rest too because tomorrow is a long day for you," she said as she stood and headed to her room.

As I walked pass Cat's bedroom heading to mine for the evening, she called out to me. "Liz, is that you," she asked as I turned and headed back to her door that was slightly cracked. "Yeah, it's me," I said lightly tapping on the door. "Come on in. I want to talk to you about something," Cat said as she sat up in the bed. She sat there quietly for a moment looking at her wedding ring before she began to speak. "Chris and I aren't doing well at all, and I don't know what else to do. I've tried to get him to go to counseling with me, but he refuses and says we are fine and we don't need counseling. He says he loves me, but he acts completely opposite. I've never told anyone this, but I think there's someone else. I've felt this way for a while now," she said as her eyes became glossy with tears. I reached over and grabbed the box of Kleenex off the dresser and consoled her. "Wow Cat. I knew something wasn't right between the two of you, but I never would've guessed this. Did you ask him if there was another woman," I questioned. After drying her eyes, she answered. "Yeah, I did on several occasions and he denied it every time. I've even considered hiring a private detective, but I hadn't been able to bring myself to do it. I guess I already know the answer," she said as she leaned back on the pillow. "It's gotten so bad that we aren't even sleeping in the same room anymore. We haven't been intimate in a while and when we are, there's no emotion from him. He never even looks at me," she said as she began crying again. "Oh Cat, I'm so sorry," I said while reaching over to hug her. "You know since Richard died, I've been in a terrible, terrible place. The thought of ending my life has crossed my mind more than once. If nothing else has come out of his death, I'm forced to seek God more during these lonely times when no one else is here to console me. So, when I feel like the world is caving in on me or when I feel there is nothing else to hold on to- I fall on my knees and cry out to God. There have been times when I could actually hear Mrs. Goodwin saying, "God is a very present help in the time of trouble. All you have to do is call out to Him." I've definitely been in a time of trouble over these last few days. Even though I'm surrounded by my dearest friends I still recognize

God is the only one who is consistently present with me to help me. "That's how you deal with this situation Cat, you turn to God. Otherwise you will lose your mind in this process. It's too much for any natural individual to deal with alone. You understand what I'm saying," I asked as I lifted her chin to get a better look. She nodded. "So, can I pray with you about this?" She nodded again and we began to pray.

I stayed there with Cat until she fell asleep. I was amazed at how I was able to console her when I, myself, was in such a desolate place. It was nothing and nobody but God who allowed me to be just what she needed at a time like this. I eased out of the bed as to not wake her and shut the door gently behind me. I could hear Celeste downstairs rambling in the kitchen, so I tipped back downstairs to see what she was up to. "Girl, why are you making so much noise down here," I asked jokingly as I flipped on the light. She had just taken the turkey out of the fridge and was preparing to make a sandwich. "Girl, I'm hungry. Why are you still up," she asked while spreading mayo on her sandwich.

Noticeably she wasn't herself. She seemed a little sluggish and definitely out of character. Celeste was always put together, at least as far as her hair and makeup was concerned. Tonight, her hair was a mess and her eyeliner had begun to run down her face causing me to believe she had been crying. "Are you okay Celeste," I asked concerned. "Yeah, I'm alright," she said as she took a huge bite out of her sandwich. I could see she wasn't fine- maybe a little drunk, but I had a long day ahead of me on tomorrow and I needed my rest, so I dared not push the matter tonight. "Well, make sure you turn off the lights before going to bed. I'll see you in the morning," I said while heading back upstairs to my bedroom.

The following morning Tangie had gotten up early and prepared breakfast for all of us. By the time I came down to the kitchen, Tangie and Cat were sitting at the table drinking coffee and munching on toast, eggs, and bacon. "Where's Celeste," I asked looking around the kitchen for her. "I guess she's still in her room asleep. She came in pretty late," Cat said as she slowly sipped on her coffee. "Yeah, when I got up to use the bathroom last night, I ran into her in the hall. She looked a hot mess," Tangie chimed in as she stood to get the jelly out of the fridge. "Yeah, I know. I ran into her in the kitchen on last night before I went to bed. I wish I knew what was going on with her. Staying out all night with random guys and coming in and sleeping until noon are definitely signs that something is going on," I said as I sat next to Tangie and poured myself a cup of coffee. No sooner had we stopped talking did Celeste walk into the kitchen. "What are you girls up to this morning," she asked as she headed to the fridge for some orange juice. "Just eating breakfast and being concerned about you. That's all," Cat said as she turned around in her chair so she could get a better look at her. "Why are y'all in my business? As if the three of you don't have enough going on in your own lives to keep you busy," Celeste said slamming the cabinet door after grabbing a glass. "Tangie, you've got more than enough going on with you and that ex-husband of yours. You would think that would be enough to keep you occupied," Celeste said as she turned to look at Cat. "And Cat, you need to be focused on those kids and that trifling, no good husband of yours. Maybe if you spent less time worrying about me and more time focusing on your marriage, your man would stay home more," she said angrily. Before any of us could address her and her angry comments, Celeste turned to me to speak her mind. "And Liz, maybe if you would've tried harder to give Richard children, he wouldn't have died from a broken heart," she said as she turned up her glass of juice to take a sip. Apparently she was angry with us about something and she'd been holding it all in and this morning she erupted. Well, she definitely accomplished what she intended- we were all shocked, hurt, and angered by her comments. "Celeste, why would you say that to us," I asked angrily. "We aren't trying to be in your business, but lately you've caused us reason to be concerned and worried. All those random guys coming by and picking you up- should we not be concerned about that," I asked as I slowly made my way to where she stood trying to hold back tears. She didn't answer, so I put my arms around her and held her until the tears began to flow. Tangie and Cat didn't move, nor did they say anything. I guess they were still angry and hurt by the comments Celeste spewed out at them.

Eventually Cat and Tangie excused themselves and went to their rooms to get dressed. It was 7:30 AM and I had to be at the funeral home to solidify Richard's funeral arrangements at 9 AM. Not only was I dealing with the drama that came with this visit from my girlfriends, but now I had to face reality once again- the reality that Richard was never coming back. As I sat behind the beautiful, cherry wood vanity Richard had given me for our fifth wedding anniversary, I began to cry. I remember when he surprised me with it. He led me into the bedroom blindfolded and whispered in my ear, "I want you to see exactly what I see when I look at you. I see a beautiful, intelligent woman who is full of life." He then removed the blindfold. "So, I decided amongst all other gifts, to get you this vanity," he whispered. Who put that much thought into gifts? Richard did! Everything he had ever given me had significance behind it. He'd sit on the end of the bed, smiling- watching me as I brushed my hair and applied my makeup. I truly missed him right now. Then a thought occurred to me- how was it possible for both my mind and heart to be members of the same body, but each have their own idea of what "reality" was? My mind knew Richard was gone and he wasn't coming back, but my heart yelled "heresy" at the mere thought of never seeing him again. It's like sitting by the phone, and in your heart happily anticipating a phone call from your deceased loved one, but knowing in your mind the call will never come- both your heart and mind accusing the other of being a liar. That's where I was in this whole thing- trying to get my mind and heart to line up and come into agreement, but my heart was putting up a really good fight and winning. My God, Richard was never coming back and I'd never be able to hold him, kiss him, talk to him, or see his smiling face ever again. What I wouldn't give to get lost in his arms, his voice, and the smell of his cologne right now.

After showering and getting dressed, I headed downstairs where Tangie, Celeste and Cat were sitting in the living room waiting for me. "You okay baby," Tangie asked as she stood and headed for the door. "Yeah, I'm okay. I had another moment," I said while searching for my keys in the bottom of my purse. "Liz, it's going to take some time, so pace yourself. There is no time schedule for grief. Everybody grieves differently but the important thing is that you allow the grieving process to happen. Don't hold back or bottle up your feelings for the sake of us. No! Let them out. We expect you to act and react just the way you are," Tangie whispered as she leaned her head down towards me forcing me to look her in the eyes. "Yeah, I hear you momma," I said sarcastically as I smiled back at her. "We're in this thing together Liz. You are not alone," Cat chimed in while heading for the front door, but not before hugging me around my neck. Surprisingly enough, Celeste even had something nice to say. "We would never let you go through this alone Liz. That's what girlfriends are for," she said as we all headed out the front door towards the car. Parker and Son's funeral home was

our next destination and I was not looking forward
to it at all.

~4~
"Watch Your Mouth"

As I stood there viewing Richard's body, I caught myself forgetting to breathe. I found myself holding my breath waiting to see Richard's chest rise and fall, but it never happened. Thinking back, most of our quality time together was spent with me lying in bed next to Richard with my head resting on his chest. I always felt so safe and secure there- no one could harm me as long as I was in his arms. Every time he inhaled, my head would rise and when he exhaled it would fall. His heart beat always sounded so loud and strong as it echoed throughout his chest. The broadness of his shoulders and his arms around me provided me a safe haven- a place for me to totally let go of all worries, cares and concerns and simply relax. Now standing here knowing I would never experience the warmth and security he provided made me absolutely sick to my stomach. "Excuse me ma'am, where is the restroom," I asked the funeral home attendant as she pointed around the corner. We couldn't wrap up the funeral arrangements fast enough. I was ready to get out of there.

After a long and tedious morning at the funeral home, my girlfriends decided to take me out to lunch with hopes of taking my mind off the earlier events of the day. They didn't understand, but no amount of food could erase the picture that had lodged itself in my mind of Richard lying there lifeless. He was always so full of life and energy. Just thinking about eating at a time like this made me even more nauseous. Now that I think about it, I hadn't really been eating much at all since Richard's death. I remember momma telling me, as a kid succumbing to peer pressure, my nerves were in my stomach. I guess she was right because since Richard's death, I hadn't been able to keep anything down and that would definitely explain why my pants had become a little loose.

Needless to say, the girls decided to take me to Malavery's Café anyway. It was the newest restaurant in Charlotte's downtown restaurant scene and supposedly it had the best Miso Salmon on the

East Coast. I was determined to eat every bit of my food and keep it down too- well for as long as I could anyway. The last thing I wanted was for my girlfriends to be worried about me not eating. "So Liz, whatcha gonna order," Cat asked as the waiter headed towards the kitchen to get our drink orders. "I think I'll try the Miso Salmon. I've been told it's really good," I said closing the menu. "That does sound good. I think I'll try it too," Cat said as she closed her menu and started rambling through her purse looking for her cell phone. The waiter finally returned with our drinks and began to take our food orders.

"So, Liz is there anything you need us to do before the home going service on Friday," Celeste asked as she took a sip of her drink. "No. You guys have done more than enough and I'm so thankful you're here with me. I don't know what I would do without you guys," I whispered as I reached over and patted Cat's hand as she was sitting the closest to me. Finally the waiter arrived with our food and for the next twenty minutes the table was completely silent.

"Liz, I forgot to tell you. Do you remember our Sunday school teacher, Mrs. Goodwin? Well, she called the house on last night and asked to speak with you, but you were in the tub so I took down her number," Tangie said while handing me a slip of paper. "She said she'd be at the funeral and she'd see you then," Tangie mentioned right before shoving another forkful of food in her mouth. "Wow. Mrs. Goodwin! We haven't seen her in over twenty years, right," Cat asked excitedly. "Yeah it has been a long time. It was good hearing from her though. She sounds exactly the same too," Tangie chuckled. "I would love to see her. She was always the go-to person with the answers and remedies for everything when we were children. I wonder if she still has those answers for life's ailments. I can't wait to see her," I said while trying my best to keep my food down. "Excuse me ladies, I have to go to the restroom," I said as I hurried from the table.

When I returned, it was obvious they had been talking about me because they all were suddenly silent when I returned to the table. "So, what or who were we talking about while I was

47

gone," I asked sarcastically while smiling. "Okay girl. We've been a little concerned about you. You've lost weight and you aren't eating," Tangie blurted out like it had been killing her to hold it in. They were absolutely right. I had lost weight. More than I would've liked to have lost. "You're right, but there's no need for concern. I am eating, and some of it manages to stay down. I think I'm going to try something light the next time, like some soup and crackers." That seemed to suffice and put their minds at ease for the moment as they stopped badgering me about my weight and went back to eating.

Later that evening, after returning home from running errands, we all ended up in the living room engrossed in small talk. "Umm, it doesn't seem as though y'all are going to say anything about it, but Celeste what in the heck got into you this morning? You must be out of your mind girl," Tangie said as she stared at Celeste. "Why on earth would you cause so much drama, especially at a time like this," Tangie asked as she shifted in her seat so she could have a better view of Celeste whenever she decided to answer. It was obvious Celeste was embarrassed about her behavior on this morning because she couldn't even look at any of us. It was apparent the rest of us were trying to let the entire thing go, but not Tangie. No she just had to bring this morning up all over again. Why did Tangie have to be so darn confrontational! "Well, I was angry! People are always whispering and talking about me and I never expected my girls- my best friends to be a part of that type of behavior," she said as she swayed her head back and forth with a hint of an attitude. "What could we have possibly done to you to make you so angry at us," I asked softly. "It's not what you did, it's what you didn't do," Celeste said as she reached for a Kleenex. "Celeste, what did we fail to do that has caused you to have so much animosity towards us," I asked as I slid to the end of my chair waiting to hear what she had to say.

It was obvious whatever was eating at Celeste ran deep. I've known this girl most of her life and what could cause her to be so angry with her friends so quickly and easily was beyond me. The only thing I could possibly associate her pain with

49

was the night she was attacked. "Y'all will never understand why I am so hurt." You weren't there when I really needed you back then," Celeste said while blowing her nose and wiping the tears from her eyes. "Why are you so angry Celeste," Tangie asked with a smidgen of curiosity and compassion in her voice. "Yeah Celeste, you can talk to us about anything. We're your girls," Cat chimed in as she attempted to console Celeste. I couldn't say anything because a huge knot had made its way from the pit of my stomach and had somehow lodged itself in my throat, preventing me from sharing what I was really hiding about the night of the attack. Talk about feeling awkward and uncomfortable. I knew where Celeste was going with this whole conversation, and truthfully, I wanted no part of it. God knows the very last thing I wanted was to dredge up old feelings about that horrible night because I did everything in my power to forget about it. Heck, we all did! Now, that entire night and all of its effects were sitting here in my living room staring me in the face, taunting me. I had to find a way out of this conversation- heck out of this room. I found myself sweating profusely and having difficulty breathing because it had become unbearable to think about the secret, my secret, possibly being revealed.

Before I could come up with an excuse to leave the room, Celeste began sharing what happened the night of the attack. "Y'all couldn't possibly understand what I've dealt with since that night," she said as she tried to regain her composure. "You can't begin to imagine how much pain I felt, both emotionally and physically," Celeste said as she began crying again. Before I could make my way over to her, Cat had already placed her arms around her to console her. "Celeste, we're so sorry for what happened to you," Cat whispered as she began to cry herself. We were all extremely uncomfortable and didn't quite know how to handle the situation as it was apparent on all our faces. Celeste proceeded to give us a little more insight on what had happened that night. The knot that had made its way to my throat had gotten even larger and even more uncomfortable by this time and now I was gasping for air. I was extremely uncomfortable hearing her recant the details of that horrible night. I never wanted to relive that night, but Celeste had already started sharing what happened. Oh how I wished someone would've covered her mouth with duct tape so she couldn't force me to hear and think about that night again.

"I am angry," Celeste spoke harshly and bluntly. "I'm angry at the men who did this to me. I'm angry at the cops for not finding them and making them pay. I'm angry at my mother for causing me to feel like there was something I did that caused the attack and for not loving me through the entire process. Most of all, I'm angry at you guys for not helping me when I needed your help the most. It seemed as though your lives continued on happily, without any interruptions and mine... well mine had come to a sudden stop." As Celeste uttered those words, our mouths fell open in disbelief. "Are you serious Celeste," Tangie asked from across the room as she stood angrily judging by the wrinkles on her forehead. "Do you really believe the three of us would've been any match for those guys," she said standing there with her hands on her hips. What was Celeste talking about? We did everything in our power to help. I, myself, turned back to help her that night, but she told me to go get help. How could she even open her mouth and voice such horrible things?

"I felt like I took the abuse, embarrassment, and shame for all of you. Since then, I've had nightmares every night," Celeste said while staring at us as she began to cry. Wow! This was a shocker for us all. We knew Celeste was angry, but never in a million years did we think it was with us and because of something we had no control over. Cat attempted to put her arms around her again, but Celeste shrugged her off. "You will never understand how I felt then and how I feel now. You will never know the suffering I endured because of that night. You will never know the hurt and pain that continues long after the horrible deed has been done," she said with such hostility and force. By this time, my internal temperature had reached its boiling point. I couldn't believe she was sitting here saying she took all the pain for us. I couldn't believe she was angry with us, like we were the ones who assaulted her. Was she not aware of how that night affected us too? Did she not realize we were all hurting because of that night as well? Heck, especially me! Before I knew it, I had forced that knot in my throat back down into the pit of my stomach and I began to share my feelings about that night. "What do you mean we don't understand how much you suffered and we don't know how much pain you endured? We know Celeste, we all know! I know better than anyone, because I was raped that night too Celeste!" Oh my God, what had I just done? It was as if my mouth was on autopilot and no matter how badly I wanted to silence it, I couldn't. There was complete silence in the room and all eyes were now on me. Did I really just say that? Surely I didn't! The secret I'd carried around and nursed like an unborn child for the last twenty-four years had just been carelessly released in an uncontrolled fit of rage. As I panned the room hoping and praying no one heard what I had just said, I soon realized they indeed had. All of them were staring at me in shock. I literally could see the backs of their throats because of how wide their mouths hung open in disbelief. How could I? Why did I? What had I done?

"Liz, what did you just say," Tangie asked with a confused look on her face as she stood and made her way towards me. I didn't answer. I couldn't answer because I too was in shock. "Liz, were you assaulted that night too," she asked while standing in front of me as she began to kneel down at my feet. "I...I... I was assaulted that night," I whispered in embarrassment and shame not just from what had happened to me, but because I hadn't confided in them about it. "Oh my God Liz, why didn't you tell us? You mean you've been carrying this thing around all this time without telling anyone," Cat whispered. "Did Richard know," Tangie asked. "No! I couldn't bring myself to tell him especially after we found out we couldn't have children. I couldn't bear to tell him we couldn't have kids because I was messed up from something that had happened to me as a child," I whispered as the tears fell from my eyes. "Oh baby, I am so sorry you dealt with this all alone," Tangie said as she hugged me and began to cry herself. "So you see

Celeste, you aren't the only one dealing with the residue of that night. I felt and I continue to feel the pain too! It was worse for me because the embarrassment and shame I experienced was self-inflicted because no one else knew about my attack. How do you break free from self-administered humiliation and degradation brought on by self? Huh Celeste, tell me," I asked while looking Celeste in her eyes. Celeste said nothing, as she was still in shock at my revelation.

Before they managed to ask me anymore questions, I excused myself and retired to my bedroom. "I can't talk about this right now. I'm going to bed," I said as I slowly stood and turned to go upstairs. I could hear them whispering, but I didn't care that their conversations were about me. I was worn out, not just from the funeral preparations but somehow releasing my secret had taken a piece of me with it, or so it felt. After showering, I climbed into bed. I never removed Richard's pillow case because it still smelled of his cologne and reminded me of him. Tonight I really needed him, so I reached for his pillow and folded it under my head, hoping to recreate his chest so I could lay on it. It didn't work though, no matter how much cologne I sprayed on it. Richard's heartbeat was the melody that put me to sleep every night since we were married and now it had been silenced forever. I eventually cried myself to sleep.

I awoke around ten thirty the next morning to a soft knock on my bedroom door. "Who is it," I asked obviously not wanting to be bothered with anymore questions from last night. "It's me Liz. Can I come in," Celeste whispered on the other side of the door. "Yeah, come on in," I said as I propped myself up against the headboard while holding Richard's pillow close to my chest. "Did I wake you," she asked feeling a little uncomfortable. "Not really. I was just sitting here thinking." Celeste slowly came in and sat at the foot of the bed. When she turned to talk to me, I could tell she had been crying. Her eyes were swollen and red and the tear tracks were still very much present on her cheeks. "What is it Celeste," I asked.

Before she could even begin to talk, she started crying again. "Liz, I had no idea you were assaulted that night too. If only I had known, then…" Celeste whispered as she began to sob even harder. "It's okay Celeste. Really I'm okay," I spoke softly as I rubbed her back. We sat there quietly for a moment and I started wondering how the two of us experienced the same horrible night but our lives took two different paths. "Well, girl we gotta get ourselves together for this funeral at three o'clock. We can't go to Richard's home going service looking like two hot messes. Richard would want us looking our very best," I said as I got up and headed to the restroom. "Yeah, you're right Liz. We gotta get ourselves together for Richard," Celeste said as she stood drying her tears and heading for the door. Before leaving the room, she turned and looked at me, "Liz, you do know I love you right." I looked up at her, smiling, and I nodded and said, "I never doubted it for a moment."

The day I dreaded had arrived. I never thought in a million years I would be burying my husband. I always pictured us growing old together. I was overcome with so many emotions- anger, sadness, and loneliness. Reality had finally set in,

Richard was never coming back. All those things we planned to do as a couple would never take place now. At that very moment, I realized something- life stopped for no one. No matter how close you were to them and no matter how much you loved them, even when they died- life didn't stop. Everyone and everything around me kept right on moving.

I promised myself I would approach this day with my best foot forward, with my game face on no matter how emotionally "jacked up" I felt inside. My girls were counting on me to be strong and I had to be strong, right? If only I could get through this funeral without breaking down, things would be tolerable. Somehow, after the attack, I had convinced myself I had to deal with reality and the "serious stuff" first and then, and only then, would I be allowed to deal with my emotions. That's how I handled everything in my life, except for my relationship with Richard. He caused me to live in the now. He taught me how to live everyday as if it were my last. With him, I dealt with my emotions as they came and I didn't put them off. But now he was gone and I had to learn to get through this time in my life without him coaching me.

After slipping into my dress, I slowly began applying my makeup. I needed to get through this without crying. While standing there applying my mascara, I could've sworn I felt Richard behind me breathing on my neck and saying what he always said, "Babe, you are already beautiful. You don't need makeup. I like you just the way you are." He would always say that right before placing his arms around me, gently kissing me on my neck and giving me the warmest, most secure hug ever. "Okay Liz! You gotta stop thinking like this or you will never get this makeup on," I spoke sternly to myself while quickly blinking my eyes in an attempt to keep the tears at bay.

I had to say a prayer before going downstairs with hopes it would strengthen me to get through this day. I placed my pillow on the floor right next to the bed and knelt on it. I rested my head on the foot of the bed where Richard and I spent so many wonderful times holding each other. "God, only you know the pain I'm dealing with right now.

Sometimes I feel like I can't take it and all I want to do is run and not have to face what's ahead of me. God, I need you to get me through this in my right mind. I miss him so much, and while I am thankful to you for the years you've given me with him- I can't help but wish I could've had more time with him. You hand crafted and tailor made that man just for me. You saved the very best for me and you allowed me many wonderful years with him. Thank you God! I pray Richard's life spoke volumes to others and their lives are changed for the better. In Jesus' name I pray, Amen," I whispered as I ended my prayer, stood, straightened my clothes and prepped myself for what was ahead as I made my way downstairs- game face and all.

I'm sure the ladies were worried about me, seeing as though I hadn't come down for breakfast, but they didn't bother me. As I slowly made my way down the stairs, there they were patiently waiting at the bottom. How would I have gotten through this thus far if they weren't here for me? They were truly my friends and I loved them dearly. No sooner had I gotten downstairs and sat on the couch did the family car arrive to take us to the church. That knot that I forced down on last night had made its way back into my throat again. It wasn't silencing any more secrets though, but it was suppressing all the emotions I was feeling from Richard's death. I wanted to yell, "I'm not going through with this! Richard isn't dead!" But that wasn't reality. Reality was, Richard was gone forever and I was headed out the door on my way to bury him.

~5~
"Goodbye and Hello"

The ride to the church seemed to be the longest I'd ever taken. It seemed even longer than the cross country road trip Richard and I took two years ago. On that particular trip, we had no concrete agenda other than to enjoy one another to the fullest. We stopped in all the little towns as we headed west, visiting all the general stores and buying little "what knots." I vividly remember watching Richard as he drove, singing and bobbing his head to Frankie Beverly and Maze. He was always a very handsome man, well put together, who knew exactly what he wanted and always had a plan to get it. That's exactly what happened with me. He wanted me and he pursued me with a well thought out plan, and it worked. I was working as a waitress at a coffee shop near the college I attended and Richard would come in every evening and flirt with me. He made it a point to always sit in the section I waited tables in. I remember him coming in one evening and sitting in the section he thought was mine, but he soon found out I wasn't waiting tables in that area. After badgering the other waitress to find out what section I was waiting tables in, he left her a tip and politely moved to my section. I watched this entire fiasco in action and I thought he was absolutely out of his mind, and I soon found out he was very persistent and completely crazy about me. Dr. Herbert, a wise instructor I once had, would often say, "The proof of desire is found in the pursuit." In other words, how badly we wanted something was demonstrated in how relentlessly we went after it. In essence, Richard desired me and he did everything in his power, no matter how crazy he looked, to obtain me. Not only did Richard win me, but more importantly- he won my heart.

As the driver pulled up in front of the church, my knees suddenly began to weaken. Friends and family lined the walkway in front of the church waiting for me to arrive. Everything in me wanted to remain right there in the car with my girls and not deal with any of this, but I had to. The driver opened the car doors and as we stepped out, we all grabbed hands and made our way towards the steps of the church. The front row of the church seemed miles and miles away. With every step we took, it seemed as though the aisle became longer and longer. Nevertheless, I made it there and planted myself right between Tangie and Cat, clenching their hands tightly.

I specifically asked that they not play any depressing or sad music at the funeral because Richard was a man full of energy and zeal. I glanced around the church to get a glimpse of how many lives Richard had touched and I was overwhelmed by the outpouring of friends, family, and loved ones. Richard was truly missed, and by the looks of things, not just by me. As I turned back around, there it was- that casket staring me in the face again. It held captive my future plans, my past and present joy and most of all- the love of my life. It was a constant reminder of all I had lost and I convinced myself life would never be joyous apart from Richard. Having sat the last ten minutes in front of the prison that held the love of my life captive, I was glad I decided on a closed casket funeral. There was absolutely no way I would've been able to sit here while seeing Richard lying there, lifeless. Truthfully a closed casket didn't make much of a difference at this point either because I knew I would never see him again. "Why me God," I whispered as I fought to hold back the tears. Tangie turned to me and squeezed my hand tighter as a simple reminder that she was here for me.

I sat there in a complete daze. I watched the mouths of everyone moving, but I heard nothing coming from them. Everything was a complete blur. The entire time sitting there, I reminisced on the things Richard and I had done and the things we laughed incessantly about. Now, more than ever, I cherished those moments we spent sitting on the couch, holding one another. One of our favorite pastimes was to sit together for hours without saying a single word. Somehow I knew what he was saying and he knew what I was saying merely from looking into each other's eyes. As long as he was in my arms, and I in his, we were perfectly okay.

The harsh thing called reality soon came crashing down again when we reached the point in the service where Richard's cousin, Lisa began to sing. As Lisa sang, I began to experience an overwhelming feeling of loneliness and brokenness, but also an assurance that I would be okay. The services were rapidly coming to an end and I wanted to say goodbye to Richard. Before the pallbearers had a chance to roll Richard's coffin down the aisle and out of the sanctuary in the vestibule, I stood and slowly made my way towards it. The church was completely silent, all except for the chords ringing from the organ in the corner. With both hands resting on the section of the coffin where I imagined his face was, I quietly whispered "Richard, you are the love of my life and you will forever remain in my heart and in my thoughts. I love and miss you so much baby. Goodbye Richard." Cat, Tangie, and Celeste were there waiting with open arms as they all embraced me. The pallbearers slowly wheeled the coffin out of the sanctuary and into the vestibule. As I exited the church, I knew life for me would never be the same again.

While sitting there in the car waiting on the funeral procession to the burial site to begin, there was a soft knock at my window. There stood Mrs. Goodwin looking as if she hadn't aged a bit. I opened the door so she could get in. "Hey ladies," she whispered as she reached out and grabbed my hand and cupped it in hers. "Hey Mrs. Goodwin," we all whispered softly and solemnly. "It's so good to see you all again, but it would've been even better under different circumstances," she said as she smiled at me. "Lizzy, I want you to know you are not alone in this. Not only do you have your girlfriends who love you dearly, but you have me as well," she spoke softly as she jotted her number down on a small piece of paper and placed it in my hands. I forgot she called me Lizzy too. The only other person who called me by that name was Richard, but hearing her refer to me that way brought a smile to my face. She gently hugged me and gave me a kiss on my forehead and blew kisses to the other ladies, before exiting the car. "We'll be in touch," she whispered as she shut the door. I slowly unfolded the small piece of paper, and realized it wasn't just her telephone number but also a scripture, "Psalm 46:1." I wasn't too familiar with that one, but I promised myself I would look it up when I returned home.

The ride to the burial site was completely quiet and it allowed me time to calm myself down as well as time to spend in prayer with God. The burial was the icing on the cake- finality. It was my last opportunity to say what was in my heart to Richard. I'd heard of people dealing with untimely deaths of loved ones, but never did I imagine how incredibly heartbroken and lost they must've felt, at least until now. I felt my life was completely out of control. I don't ever remember feeling this lonely before- not even when mom and dad died. "God, you have to help me! I'm falling apart here. Why did you have to take Richard from me? We were so happy," I pleaded as I whispered to God in prayer. Cat reached over and gently patted me on my knee. Before I knew it, we were pulling up at the burial site. Cat, Tangie, and Celeste had already exited the car and the driver was standing at my door with his hand extended to assist me. I slowly exited the car and there they were- all three of them again- waiting patiently as they had done through this entire nightmare. I reached down and placed my hand on my stomach because it had started to bother me again. Tangie obviously realized what was happening and she reached into her bag and handed me a mint.

As the pastor performed the graveside service, my mind began to wander again. I thought to myself, "what a beautiful sunny day it is. The sky is remarkably clear and blue." The last time I saw a sky this clear and blue was when Richard and I went to Barbados on our fifth year wedding anniversary. He was always the master of surprises. Richard refused to tell me where we were headed until we arrived at the airport. I remember that evening like it was yesterday- I had come home from grocery shopping to a living room full of luggage. "Richard, where are you? Why are all these suitcases in the front room," I shouted up the stairs. He came down with the biggest smile on his face. "We're going away for our anniversary babe," he said as he embraced me. "What," I said confused but excited as well. He knew I had requested some time off from work causing my two day weekend to be extended into a five day weekend. I thought we were going to spend the week tucked away in our home, but he had done it once again- surprised me. He wouldn't tell me where we were going, but he did say he had packed my suitcase with clothing for warmer weather. Our plane was scheduled to leave the very next morning. He had planned another surprise for me in our own home for the night as well. He removed the grocery bags from my arms, sat them on the floor at the foot of the stairs, and escorted me upstairs where he had drawn a warm, bubble bath for me complete with candles and rose petals. I was blown away, yet again. "Babe, I want you to think about absolutely nothing while you're relaxing in your bath. I have it all under control," he said smiling as he watched me undress and then helped me into my bath. "I'll return in thirty minutes to help you out. Enjoy sweetie," Richard whispered as he exited the bathroom singing.

As promised, Richard returned and helped me out of the tub where he waited with a towel and my robe. One of the things I loved most about Richard was his patience. Seeing me completely nude obviously excited him, but he saw no need in trashing the plans he'd made and rushing the evening. Richard knew I was his wife for life and I wasn't going anywhere. As I entered the bedroom, there on the bed, Richard had placed a beautiful, silk and lace gown. Wow, this man surely knew how to make me smile and my intention was to make him smile before the night was out. He waited patiently as I slipped into the gown, and then he escorted me downstairs where my ears were immediately greeted by the soft and sensual sounds of jazz. My nose was aroused by the smell of an awesomely seasoned dish that had obviously been prepared while I was bathing. When we turned the corner to enter the dining room, there before my eyes was a table set for two- candlelight and all. Standing next to the table, uniformed completely in white, was the chef Richard had hired for the evening. He smiled at me as he nodded his head to say hello. Richard gently pulled my chair out and waited for me to sit and he then proceeded to his chair on the other side of the table. I was completely blown away and never in a million years would I have expected this.

After dinner, Richard softly grasped my hand and helped me from my chair as he ushered me into the living room where the lights were dimmed and candles were illuminated throughout. The coffee table had been removed and the floor was covered in what looked like hundreds of rose petals. He then turned to me and said, "May I have this dance beautiful?" I nodded feeling like a school girl who had just been asked to the prom by the handsomest guy in school. We danced for what seemed like hours- our bodies moving perfectly in unison with one another and the music. I loved that man and everything he stood for. Now here I was sitting at his graveside with so many unanswered questions.

I never thought about what I would do when and if I was faced with having to say goodbye to my lover, best friend, and soul mate. Who plans for this? As the pastor ended the graveside service, I stood and slowly walked towards Richard's casket. I gently placed a small, red sachet filled with the dried petals from the roses Richard had covered our living room floor with. "Goodbye my love. We will meet and dance again. I will absolutely love you, forever," I whispered as I turned and slowly began to walk towards the car. Tangie, Cat, and Celeste soon followed suit as we walked hand in hand.

I now had to plan my life alone. No more Richard, no more plans of growing old together. As I fiddled around in my purse looking for a tissue, I found the note Mrs. Goodwin had given me with the passage of scripture she had written on it. The car we were riding in had a bible in the back pocket of the seat right in front of me. I quickly opened the bible and turned to Psalm 46:1 and it read, "God is our refuge and strength, always ready to help in times of trouble." Wow! How fitting was this passage of scripture. I was definitely in a time of trouble and I desperately needed help. Not only was I troubled and in pain, but I had become sick in my soul as well. I continued to read, "So we will not fear when earthquakes come and the mountains crumble into the sea." I truly felt my world was coming to an end. I was experiencing inner turmoil and I didn't know how to get free of it. I was so glad Mrs. Goodwin had come to the funeral. I desperately needed to speak with her again. Maybe

I would call her tomorrow after my doctor's appointment and talk about this overwhelming feeling of loneliness and sadness I was suddenly succumbing to.

~6~
"Emotional Roller Coasters"

After the services were over, Tangie, Celeste, and Cat came back to the house where we sat silently in the living room for what seemed like hours. It was finally starting to sink in now- Richard was gone for good. Eventually Tangie headed towards the kitchen. She was always the "mother hen" of the group. I knew exactly what she was up to. She was headed to fix us all something to eat, but who could eat at a time like this? I'd definitely try my best, but my stomach had been in knots all day. After about thirty minutes, Tangie returned to the dining room with four bowls and my big stock pot full of some concoction she hooked up. When did she have time to cook? Whatever it was, it smelled good. We all made our way to the table as Tangie headed back into the kitchen to get some saltines. She'd gotten up after everyone had fallen asleep on last night and prepared vegetable beef soup. After sitting, she began spooning soup into our bowls and when she reached mine, she spooned only a little in my bowl. "Liz, I want you to take it slow. I know you've been nauseous lately and I don't want you to overdo it. If you feel you can handle more, then by all means go for it." "Yes ma'am mom," I whispered with a smirk on my face. We all laughed. It felt good smiling again and it felt even better to see them smiling again.

Before I could finish the first bowl of soup, my stomach gave a loud warning sign. I didn't eat nearly as much as I or Tangie would've hoped for, but we were both glad for the small amount I managed to retain. We chatted here and there as the evening progressed, but we spent most of the evening in our rooms. While sitting at the vanity Richard had surprised me with one year, I knew I had to move forward. If I was ever going to be happy again in life, I had to make some changes- starting tonight. So finally, I decided to remove Richard's pillowcase and replace it with another one. It being covered in his cologne was the reason I hadn't removed it before. It was the next best thing, in my mind, to having him here with me. Of course

77

I cried throughout the entire process, but it would help me eventually. I reached over on Richard's side of the bed and removed his bible from the nightstand. Instead of reading mine tonight, I decided to read his.

I found myself in so much turmoil since Richard's death, so I decided to read some notes from a message Pastor Marcie had taught on soul restoration. During the message she explained our souls were the "seats" of our emotions. If that were true, then my soul was definitely in a hot seat and desperately in need of restoration. My soul had taken up a new residency smack dab in the middle of "Emotionville" and I was quickly becoming all too familiar with this place. The only other time I can remember experiencing such an overwhelming bout of emotions was the night I was assaulted. Back then, emotions I never knew I possessed came spewing out of me at the most inopportune time. Now here I was again experiencing what felt like déjà vu. I didn't handle my emotions well at all back then. I took them and tucked them away nicely in an internal locked box and I never dealt with them ever again- until now of course. When I finally did share the events of that night, so much internal damage had already taken place. "I have to talk to someone or I'm going to lose my mind," I whispered while looking up from my notes. The effects of that night were still haunting me and even more so now that the others knew my secret.

There was a knock at the door. "It's me Liz," Tangie whispered as she turned the knob and entered the room. "Hey. How are you feeling," she asked as she sat at the foot of the bed where she studied me. She knew me all too well. "I'm okay. My stomach is still a little upset, but I'm okay." "Okay, I was just checking on you. So when is your doctor's appointment again," she asked solely to remind me that I had one scheduled. "Don't worry Tangie, my appointment is at 10 AM tomorrow morning and I will be there. I'll call you as soon as I'm done. Okay?" Tangie nodded and smiled at me before patting me on my foot, whispering goodnight, and leaving the room. You'd assume Tangie would have a house full of kids considering how motherly she was with us, but she didn't. She never even talked about having children, so we made the assumption she never wanted any. My eyelids began to get heavy and I started yawning every other minute like clockwork. There were parts of my notes I'd forgotten I had read because I kept nodding off in the midst of reading them. "Time to call it quits," I thought to myself as I tucked the notes inside Richard's bible. I needed to get some rest because my girls were leaving to go home in the morning and I had a doctor's appointment as well. Before turning off the lamp, I knelt down on Richard's side of the bed, where we knelt every night together, and I prayed.

Before I could get back into bed, there was another knock at the door. It was Cat. Judging by the look on her face, something was wading heavily on her mind, but what? "Cat, is everything okay," I asked as I tried to make sense of the emotion evident on her face. "I'm fine," she said before exhaling harshly. "No I am not okay and I'm tired of always pretending that I'm fine, knowing life is pure hell for me," she said forcefully as she exhaled. I sat there with my mouth open because I'd never seen Cat act in this manner before. "Cat, what is going on with you? How is your life pure hell," I asked confused. She had two beautiful children and she still had the option, if she wanted to, to embrace her husband but I didn't. "Liz, life for me has been horrible for the past few years. Chris is barely home and all the household and parenting responsibilities have fallen on me. I'm always tired and worn out when I get home from work and the kids are there waiting on me to help with homework. Who knew you could be surrounded by so many people and still feel so very lonely," she whispered as she grabbed my hands while looking me in my eyes. While Cat vented, I sat there in disbelief. I knew life for her had to be hard considering Chris wasn't functioning in his fatherly and husbandly roles, but I had no idea it was this bad. Here she was sitting on my bed, in tears, pouring out her heart to me and all I could think of was how much I wish I had Richard here to fuss with right now. "Cat, I knew things between you and Chris were rough, but I had no idea they were this bad. What are you going to do," I asked as I slid closer to her while placing my arms around her to console her. "I don't know Liz, but what I do know is I'm tired of living this way. I'm tired of pretending all is well when my house is in shambles. No one at my church has a clue of how absolutely horrible my home life is," she said as she tried to regain her composure. "And to make matters worse, I'm attracted to someone else," she said as she turned to see my response to what she had just said. I knew I hadn't heard what I thought I heard. What did she say? Did she just say she liked someone else? "Cat what exactly do you mean you're attracted to someone else? You haven't been with another man have you," I asked not really sure I wanted to know the answer. She paused for a moment, "Don't worry Liz. I haven't been with him." Whew! That was the best piece of news I'd heard in a while. "So what have you done with him," I asked sarcastically but seriously wanting the truth. She told me they talked and confided in one another about their lives and the issues in them. Michael was his name and according to Cat, he has made this whole process with Chris tolerable. I was no rocket scientist, but this only seemed to make matters a little more murky and complicated to me. I didn't feel that now was the time for us to discuss the "Michael" situation. She was hurting and I was tired. We would definitely talk about Michael again and really soon, but for now- my bed was calling me. Before she left the room, she calmed down and I gave her a hug and told her how much I loved her and that I was praying for her, Chris, and the children.

It hadn't been twenty minutes before there was another knock at the door. I thought maybe Cat had left something of hers and was returning to get it, but I was wrong. It was Tangie at the door. She heard crying coming from my room and she peeped in to make sure I was okay. "I'm okay Tangie," I said while rolling my eyes and smiling at her. "Alright, I was just checking," Tangie whispered. As I stared at her, I realized I couldn't recall a time when I ever saw her cry. Tangie was always so tough and reserved, and I thought a lot of it had to do with her never wanting anyone to think she needed them. But at some point in our lives, we've all played the "need" game and there was absolutely nothing wrong with needing help. "Hey. Can I ask you something," I whispered. Tangie stopped, turned and nodded yes before exiting the room. "I've never seen you cry? This may sound a little crazy, but do you ever feel anything," I asked while sitting up on the bed so I could hear her clearly. "Yeah, I get emotional Liz, but just not that often. I'm a very emotional person. I just choose not to show it all the time," she said in her "matter of fact" voice which was usually a sign that she was done discussing the matter. "Okay Tangie. I'm just asking. I know you've been concerned about me, but I've been concerned about you as well." Tangie did her very best to convince me all was well with her and I was way too tired to argue with her about it, so eventually we said our goodnights and she left the room quietly. Tomorrow had to be much better, or so I would tell myself until it turned out that way. Eventually I settled down and the last thing I remembered before falling asleep was twirling Richard's wedding band around my thumb and whispering, "I miss you babe."

~7~
"But It Feels So Good"
(Cat's Words Exactly)

I awoke this morning anxious to see my babies. CJ and Sarah had never been away from me this long, but they were with their father and hopefully they were enjoying themselves. My flight was scheduled to leave the airport heading back to DC at noon. "Tooth brush- check. Make-up bag- check," I whispered as I went down my mental checklist, while plundering through my luggage making sure I had everything packed. After glancing up at the clock, I realized I had a few minutes before the cab arrived, so I decided to peep in on Liz. I knocked on the door, but there was no answer. Then it hit me, her doctor's appointment was scheduled for 10 AM this morning. "I'll give her a call once I land in DC," I thought to myself. I sure hope her appointment went well. God knows that girl couldn't handle any more bad news right now. As I turned and headed for my room, I heard the cab driver impatiently blowing the horn downstairs.

Grabbing my suitcase and purse, I hurried down the stairs and out the door to the cab waiting to take me to the airport.

I couldn't get the thought of Michael out of my head, much less out of my soul. I thought about him the entire ride to the airport. Every time he crossed my mind, it brought a huge grin to my face. I'd never met anyone who knew me so well or anyone who had the innate capability of bringing out emotions I wasn't even aware I possessed. It was like we knew each other inside and out. We had the same interests, he was very attentive to my needs, and he hung onto every word I said. That in itself was a breath of fresh air considering what I was accustomed to from my husband, Chris. Michael constantly told me how smart I was and how much I inspired him, but Chris never paid attention to anything I said or did. I must admit the compliments and flattery sounded and felt great, not to mention he was such a driven and determined person, much like myself. There isn't anything wrong with a little flattery, right? Compliments and flattery were things I'd gone without for far too long and considering Michael and I had been dear friends since college- compliments meant so much more coming from him. This was the first time I'd ever been involved in something that felt so good, but deep down inside I knew it wasn't good for me. I couldn't stop my feelings, nor could I let go of this deep hearted friendship we'd created. The entire relationship was like poison to my soul, but one I willingly and eagerly drank. Every inch of me wanted Michael in my life, but my head fiercely and violently yelled, "No, let him go! This isn't good for you!" I felt like I was living in a fantasy with Michael. Then suddenly life and marriage snatched me back to reality- a living hell. Marriage was a consistent drought that left me parched and thirsty for love, companionship, and conversation all the time. I knew my marriage was far from being okay and now I wasn't so sure I wanted it to be okay. The closeness and familiarity I had with Michael made for hours and hours of enjoyable and exciting conversation. There was never a time we found ourselves at a loss for words because we always had lots to talk about. As far as I was concerned, everything Chris lacked as a husband Michael more than made up for. No matter how much I knew I needed to let Michael go, I absolutely couldn't bring myself to do so. He managed to fill a void I'd experienced most of my life. The deprivation I'd experience was due in part to my father's lack of being involved in the matters of the house when I was a child. I watched my mother do everything from paying the bills to cutting the grass and my father never had any input. His absence of input wasn't solely because my mother wouldn't allow it, but also because he didn't want it. As kids when we wanted anything, instead of asking my father- we would ask my mother. It was understood she was in charge of the finances. So as I matured, I unknowingly repeated the same behavior I saw demonstrated in my house as a child. Most of the time, daddy wasn't there and when he was, he expected my mother to handle everything and mom was perfectly okay with doing so. Yeah, it was twisted and dysfunctional, but it was our reality and I soon carried that same reality right into my relationship and marriage to Chris.

Michael was just the opposite though. He was a man who took charge and understood his authority as a man. He knew exactly what he wanted and he made it known. There was an authoritative way about him that made him extremely attractive to me. I would never admit it to him or anyone else, but this characteristic in him is what I found the most appealing. I secretly wanted a man to lead- to tell us what we would and would not do as a family. I wanted a man- my man to lead. I wanted a man who was capable of taking charge in any situation, and Michael fit the bill. There was always something absolutely wonderful about a man who walked in his authoritative strength. You know that kind of man that didn't just handle things in the workplace, but he handled them at home as well. One whose body language and everything associated with him yelled, "No worries babe. I got this." There was nothing more exciting and secure to me than a deliberate man- one who wasn't afraid to strut confidently with his shoulders squared, his eyes fixed, and his steps sure and steady. I'd grown tired of handling everything in my home and even though it was partially my fault, my shoulders had grown tired of carrying the load. I wanted to put the load down, but Chris was in no position to pick it up. I wanted a respite and Michael provided it for me. I'm a decent God-fearing woman and I deserve to be happy too, right? After all, Michael and I weren't doing anything other than talking and encouraging one another. There was no harm in that, right? Even though I would never admit it to anyone, this seemingly innocent relationship had me totally consumed- mind, body, and soul. So much so until the very things I found important before, no longer seemed that important to me anymore. Michael made me feel alive, intelligent, beautiful, and most of all desired. I'd been void of this for far too long and even though everything within me kicked against where this relationship with Michael was headed, I wasn't ready to let it go.

How did it come to this, I questioned myself. I'd been lacking "true" companionship for a very long time, but Chris never seemed to be lacking anything. I believe he was receiving companionship elsewhere. I tried to convince Chris to come to counseling with me on several occasions, but he never saw a need for us to go. If you let him tell it, our marriage was fine. Chris was a master at picking a fight with me, which usually ended with him storming out of the house and staying out all night. Nothing I did or said ever seemed to please him and not to mention the countless excuses he made about where he was and who he was with. Deep down inside I knew Chris was involved with someone else, and truthfully- I really didn't care. Somehow I felt his infidelity had given me the okay or the license to pursue Michael further. My connection with Michael was the best thing that had happened to me in a long time and I, by no means, was about to give it up now. I definitely wasn't giving up the relationship for my ungrateful, dishonest husband. I needed this relationship with Michael! But I would be lying if I didn't admit there was an inner voice doing everything to get my attention- to get me to listen. I chose to ignore it because I was willing to pay whatever cost to hold on to this relationship with Michael. No, not even the lofty price of my sanity, morals, and family was enough to cause me to turn loose the relationship we'd developed.

The cab driver stopped in front of the airport, got out of the cab, and opened my door as he headed for the trunk to remove my luggage. After reaching into my purse for money to pay the driver, I grabbed my rolling luggage and headed inside the airport towards the Delta counter. Just as I reached the counter, my cell phone rang. While the clerk weighed my bags, I answered the call. "Hello," I whispered softly because I hated when people talked on their cell phones in public places especially while being waited on. Now here I was doing the exact same thing. "Hey kid," the voice whispered on the other end. It was Michael and I was excited, grinning from ear to ear. It was both cute and playful hearing Michael refer to me as "kid." It not only made me feel young but also vibrant. I hadn't spoken to him in two days and it was good hearing his voice again. "Hey you," I whispered with a huge grin on my face. "Can you hold for a moment Michael," I asked as I finished my transaction with the clerk and headed to the security check point.

"Okay, I'm back," I spoke softly while navigating my way through the tons of people as I headed to the check point. "I hadn't spoken to you in a few days and I wanted to see how things were with you and your girlfriends in Charlotte," he whispered in that voice that always made me grin even harder. "Things went well. I'm actually getting ready to board the plane in a few moments heading back home." "Oh, okay. You're on your way home huh," he asked with a hint of sarcasm in his voice. "Yeah! I'm ready to get back and see my babies. I've really missed them." "Well, okay then. I was calling to check on you, that's all. Have a safe flight and give me a call when you get a moment. Okay sweetie?" "Sure. You know I will. Talk with you soon Michael," I said as I hung up the phone grinning like a Cheshire cat.

It never failed. Every time I spoke with him, I enjoyed the conversation immensely, but once I hung up I felt absolutely divided internally. I felt like a teenager who was sneaking around behind her mother's back and doing something she had been told not to do. But no matter how torn I felt after speaking with Michael, I always managed to shake it off and look forward to the next time I would speak with him. "Flight three hundred and two is now boarding at gate five heading to Washington, DC," the attendant spoke loudly over the intercom. "That's my flight," I whispered to myself as I hurried to get in line to board the plane. I spent the entire forty-five minutes of the flight home playing the "what if" game in my mind. You know, "What if Michael wanted more from our friendship? What if we were romantically involved?" Those "what if" games were fantasies that had managed to infiltrate my reality and they became even more desirable as time went on. As soon as the plane landed at BWI airport, I phoned Chris to come and pick me up. "Hey babe, I'm here. Can you come get me now?" "Dang babe! I just ran out to the store to get a few things. I don't think I'll be able to make it there to get you. Can't you call a cab or something," Chris questioned in a nonchalant tone. Wow, he couldn't even come pick his wife up from the airport. "Are you serious Chris? Fine, but where are the kids," I asked angrily. "Oh yeah, I dropped them at your mom's on last night. They were begging to stay the night at their Nana's house." "Alright Chris. I'll see you when I get home," I said as I hung up the phone. This was exactly the type of mess that made my marriage to Chris feel like a living hell. Michael would never leave me stranded at the airport because I meant too much to him. Yeah, Michael was the type of guy that would be waiting for me when my plane landed, or so I'd convinced myself. I knew my husband very well and Chris was not coming home until later tonight, if then. I had begun to regret coming home, but I'm sure the sight of my babies would change that and brighten my day. The cab dropped me off in front of my house, but I didn't go inside. All I could think about was seeing CJ and Sarah. So I put my luggage in the trunk of my car and backed out as I headed over to my mom's house.

No sooner did I turn the corner onto my mom's street did a smile come across my face. The kids were in the yard playing with the kids from next door and when they saw my car they started jumping up and down and yelling, "Momma's home! Momma's home!" I can't begin to explain how happy I was after seeing their reactions to me coming down the road. If there was no one else on the face of this earth I knew unconditionally and absolutely loved me, I knew my children did. Before I could get out of the car, Sarah made her way around to the driver's side and climbed in my lap and began kissing me on my face. "Hey baby! I'm glad to see you too," I whispered as I hugged her tightly. CJ was always so reserved in demonstrating "mushiness" in front of others. He walked over to me, after I'd gotten out of the car, and he gently put his arm around my waist, "Hey momma." Those who knew CJ understood this small gesture spoke volumes. I leaned down and kissed him on the top of his head and said, "I missed you too baby." It felt great to be home and see my babies.

Mom stepped out onto the porch to see what all the commotion was about. "Hey girl," she yelled with a big grin on her face as she sat down in the first available patio chair. "Hey mom," I said climbing the stairs as I sat across from her. "Have the kids been behaving themselves," I asked while watching Sarah and Kimmie make mud pies on the steps just below us. "Oh Cat, they have been on their best behavior since Chris dropped them off the night you left for Charlotte," she whispered right before taking another sip of her lemonade. "What! Mom, what did you say? Chris brought them to you on last night, right," I asked as the hairs on the back of my neck stood up from anger. "No baby," she said with a confused look on her face. "Chris brought the kids to me right after he dropped you off at the airport. He said you changed your mind and you thought the kids would enjoy being at my house while you were gone as opposed to staying at the house with him. You know I thought something was a little weird about that because I knew you would've at least called me and told me of the change in plans," mom mentioned while still looking confused but content. Wow! Chris lied to me the entire time. He had me believing the kids were with him while I was away. "Well, tell me this mom, did you take Sarah to her recital," I asked hoping for an answer I knew I wasn't about to get. "Well baby, Chris brought Sarah's recital clothes with him when he dropped them off. He mentioned he had an appointment the night of the recital and he asked me to take her. Of course I agreed," she whispered sounding like she was about to be chastised for doing so. It was one thing that Chris never had time for me, but now he didn't even have time for his kids.

I had heard enough. "Come on kids and get your stuff. It's time to go home," I said as I stood and straightened my clothes. "Mom, thank you so much for being here for me and the kids. I love you," I whispered before bending down and hugging her neck and kissing her forehead. "Cat, don't do anything crazy when you see Chris. You hear me," she said with concern in her voice. "Don't worry mom. I won't," I assured her as the kids and I headed to the car. I was silent the entire ride home. How could he drop off our kids like sacks of dirty laundry? What was going on with him? I couldn't wait to confront him about the lies, the deceit, and the mystery woman I knew he was involved with.

Immediately my mind wandered back to Michael. I wondered what he was doing. Was he thinking about me? I wanted to text him or call him, but my kids were in the car. I'm sure if Michael had kids, he would never have treated them the way Chris treated ours. Before I knew it, I had begun the "what if" games again. These games had started to become a little dangerous, not to mention time consuming but I couldn't stop my mind from wandering. They had become dangerous because I found myself actually pondering how I could make my thoughts reality. These games had become time consuming because not only did they affect my mind, but I put so much energy into mentally formulating them that I was too tired to do much else. I wanted more than anything to be happy, but happiness alone wasn't the answer. I had experienced happiness before in the past, but happiness never lasted long. There was so much to talk about, not just with Chris but with Michael as well. I constantly daydreamed of a life with Michael, but once again I couldn't manage to keep my head silent on the matter. It kept butting in with consequences and repercussions and I didn't want to hear any of that. I couldn't let go of Michael, nor the fantasy life I had dreamt about each and every night after our reconnection. No matter how hard I tried, I absolutely couldn't get Michael out of my heart, out of my head, and out of my soul. I was now totally infatuated with him and now faced with a huge dilemma. Which member of my body was I to follow, my head or my heart? My head knew the right thing to do. I'd attended church almost all my life and I knew all about adultery and emotional strongholds. Oh, but my heart didn't care anything about what my upbringing entailed. No, my heart wanted Michael at all costs and I, slowly but surely, began to throw all caution to the wind with hopes of living out my fantasy with him. Both my head and heart had convincing cases, but only one would be victorious.

~8~
"Swallowed Up By Secrets"
(Celeste's Dark, Twisted Mind)

Finally, my plane landed and I was hoping Cat's flight had arrived and that she had already been picked up. Some would think that what I'm doing is wrong and just downright scandalous, but I'm only taking what I deserve. I deserve to be happy- yes even at the expense of others. "Hey baby," he said as he kissed my cheek and took my luggage. "How was your trip," he asked as we walked to the car he had waiting just outside the door. "It was okay. You know I had several run-ins with Tangie. She must be one miserable chic to always be trying to pick fights with me," I said as I waited for him to open the door for me to get in. As he was putting my luggage in the trunk, I pulled the mirror down to make sure my makeup looked flawless and it did. When he opened the door and got into the car, he leaned over and gave me a tender kiss on my lips. As always, he was excited to see me. "Well, I'm glad you're home. How about that," he said as he reached over and squeezed my knee gently. "I'm glad to be home," I whispered with a slight hint of remorse. Even though I tried to convince myself that what I was doing wasn't wrong, there was still a small voice deep down inside of me that wouldn't shut up. No matter how much I talked about what I was doing and how much I acted as if it didn't bother me, the truth of the matter was- it did! I was only taking care of and preserving self though. Yeah, that was it. I was preserving myself at all costs. No one ever looked out for Celeste not now and definitely not back then when I was attacked as a child.

Even though I was extremely skilled at convincing others that what I was doing was absolutely okay, there was always one person who seemed to always see right through the puffs of smoke I was blowing and I could never fool her. That person was me. I was too far out there now and at this point, there was no turning back. I had to continue to talk the talk and walk the walk in order to maintain the level of living I had accumulated up until this point. How did I let myself get tied up and tangled up in this web? The way I originally thought I would feel isn't how I felt at all. At some point in this game of life, I lost track of who I was and what I stood for. I can remember at some point, feeling strongly about specific morals and values, but they became mere puffs of smoke that had since evaporated. The sad part is I can't even remember at what point I vanished and this shell of a person appeared. But I'm "neck" deep in it now and there is no way I can retreat- I'm stuck! "Are you hungry babe," he asked sincerely concerned about me and my well being, sometimes even more so than I was about myself. "No babe, I'm okay. I ate before I boarded the plane," I whispered before allowing my memories to take me adrift to my childhood again.

"Celeste, are you sure you didn't cause this on yourself," mom questioned a few weeks after I was attacked. What could an innocent twelve year-old possibly have done to entice the men that attacked her? I couldn't believe what I was hearing. Surely this wasn't how mothers console and comforted their children, was it? How could my mother accuse me of teasing the guys who raped me? She was beginning to sound just like all the others. "I knew that little girl was fast. She was probably already having sex," is what they would whisper when I walked by and they thought I wasn't listening. I knew exactly what those piercing stares meant. Talk about the heaviness of shame and embarrassment weighing you down. That's exactly what I endured as an innocent twelve year old child. The burden of that shame and embarrassment was so heavy then and it manages to be even heavier now. I've never been able to lay that burden down, even until today.

"Babe, did you hear me," he asked as he pulled the car off to the side of the road. I was so caught up in my thoughts I didn't realize he had been talking to me. When I turned to address him, he realized I had been crying. "What's wrong Celeste" he whispered as he began to wipe the tears from my face. "I'm okay," I said as I cleared my throat and proceeded to remove my makeup compact from my purse. How could I have let this happen again? I promised myself I would never let a man see me vulnerable ever again. The moment they got wind of your weaknesses, they pounced on you and used it to your demise. I promised I would never let a man see me sweat or cry, for that matter, ever again. "Can you stop by the drug store on the corner by my house," I asked as I covered the last tear track with my makeup. He was the one and only man I had ever allowed to console me after that horrible night as a child. Every other man was, what I considered, pawns in my game because I never trusted them enough to allow them close to me. I often wondered why I allowed him in and no one else. Maybe it had something to do with the fact that he belonged to another and I felt I never had to worry about commitment issues with him. Yeah, that was it. Even though he was committed to someone else, his heart, body and soul belonged to me and I took full advantage of it.

After pulling up in front of the drug store, he proceeded to get out the car and open the door for me, but I stopped him. "Babe, I think I'll go in by myself," I whispered while touching his shoulder to stop him before he was able to get out. "Okay. I'll be here when you get done", he said while sitting back in his chair and closing the door. Once I entered the store, I quickly headed to the counter. "Excuse me ma'am. What aisle are your razors on," I whispered. "They're on aisle nine on the right" the cashier said as she pointed towards the back of the store. The very last thing I wanted was for him to come in and see me buying razors. I promised him I had stopped, but I hadn't. In fact my habit had gotten worse. My God if anyone ever found out... well, they would never understand why I do it. I'm embarrassed myself, but I can't stop. After grabbing the razors and a box of Kleenex to hide what I had actually come into the store to get, I headed to the counter to pay. He was waiting for me right there in the same spot as promised. "You okay," he asked trying to figure out why I was so fidgety. "I'm fine babe. Just a little tired." I dare not tell him what was really going on with me.

I couldn't get to my house quickly enough. I had the shakes because I needed to release and it had been too long since the last time. I was feeling very anxious and I couldn't focus at all. I was praying he didn't ask to come in. "Celeste, do you mind if I come in for a little while," he asked as he pulled into my driveway. I really wanted to spend some time with him, but not as much as I wanted to release this tension and pressure I was feeling. "No, not today babe. I'm really tired from my flight. Maybe tomorrow," I whispered as I rubbed his thigh hoping he would understand. I started feeling a little dizzy as I stood after getting out of the car. It seemed with every step I took towards my house, my front door got farther and farther away. I'd never experienced withdrawals to this extent, but I had never gone this long without a fix either. I was tempted to release while I was with the girls in Charlotte, but I was too afraid they would find out about my secret, so I didn't.

I finally reached the door and after putting the key in the knob, I turned to wave goodbye. No sooner than I was inside, did I drop everything but the pack of razors and darted towards the bathroom while ripping them open with my teeth. Everything from this point forward seemed to be moving extremely slow. Have you ever experienced a state in which your mind continued moving normally, but for some reason everything else around you had slowed to the pace of a snail? I'd never experienced anything like this before. I felt like someone had lit a bonfire on the inside of me, but my skin was cool and clammy to the touch. Surely this was due in part to my not being able to get a fix while away with the girls. Once inside the bathroom, I pushed the door closed and leaned against it as I slid down it until my bottom rested on the cold tile floor. Finally, I was about to get some relief! It had been way too long that I'd been carrying around all this tension, stress, and pressure. Releasing it was all I found myself thinking about, so much so until the "shakes" had set in. I'd managed to calm myself down enough to gently press the razor against my skin and as I slowly and softly slid it across my wrist- there was instantaneous relief. Suddenly everything was still and silent and I could literally hear my heart beating rapidly in my chest. "Ahhhh," what a release I felt as the warm blood streamed from my wrist, down my hand- forming a pool on the floor. Just as fast as the relief came did it leave just as quickly. It didn't matter this time because I had been holding it for far too long and any amount of relief was very much appreciated at this point.

After sitting there for at least ten minutes, I began squeezing my wrist in an attempt to apply pressure so the blood flow would stop. I pulled myself up on my knees and eventually stood by pulling up using the sink. I quickly reached to get some gauze from the medicine cabinet before the blood started to flow again. I had mastered cutting so to the point that I no longer worried about bleeding to death or cutting major arteries. After all the trial and error sessions I'd experienced, I knew exactly where to cut and how deeply to cut. Sadly enough, I had become a pro at mutilating myself and the initial pain I felt from piercing my skin with the razor no longer affected me. After wrapping my wrist in gauze and cleaning up the blood on the floor, I made my way to the bed.

Every time I was silent and still, my mind would wander back to that horrible night when I was twelve. No matter how much I tried to get that night out of my mind, I couldn't. When I closed my eyes I could feel their hands all over me and I wanted it to stop. I begged and I pleaded with them to let me go. I tried assuring them that if they let me go, I would tell no one but they wouldn't listen. The look in their eyes only confirmed what I knew was about to happen to me. How does a twelve year-old brace herself for the most horrific moment in her life? I couldn't have begun to fathom the pain, disgrace, and humiliation I was about to endure at the hands of those evil, malicious, and disgusting men.

I saw Liz coming back to help me after she was able to get free. But she would never have been a match against the three of them, so I told her to run fast and get help. They literally dragged me, kicking and screaming, further into the woods where they snatched my clothes off and proceeded taking turns performing their evil deeds. I can't begin to explain the pain I felt. It was unbearable and at that very moment I wanted to die so I could escape what was happening to me. The things they said to me were things that I had only read about or heard in movies. They cursed me, abused me, and treated me like a piece of trash that they merely tossed away when they were done.

When Tangie's dad finally found me, I was exhausted from trying to fight them off. I remember feeling so safe in his arms while he whispered, "It's going to be okay baby. It's going to be okay," as he carried me back to the house. Tangie's brothers followed behind in shock. I was in so much pain until I wasn't able to sit, so he laid me down on the couch and sent Tangie to get a blanket to cover me as he called the police and my mom. I remember the scared faces of the three of them- Tangie, Cat, and Liz- as they sat on the chair across from me crying just as hard as I was. Eventually, they managed to build up enough courage to come over and begin to pick the leaves and dirt from my hair and console me.

The cops finally showed up and asked me a few questions before they headed to the scene of the assault. My mom finally made it to Tangie's house so she could go to the emergency room with me. I tried to walk to the car, but it was too painful. So Tangie's dad carried me and buckled me in right before he kissed me on my cheek and promised me it would all be okay. When we arrived at the hospital, mom went in and got a wheelchair so I wouldn't have to walk. I'll never forget the looks on the faces of the people in the emergency room as my mom wheeled me down the hall to the room that was waiting for me. Their looks were those of suspicion, speculation, and confusion. That was the very first time I had experienced embarrassment and shame after the attack. Even though most of them weren't aware of what had taken place a few hours earlier, their looks and whispers made me think they did.

The officer who had come to the house had also followed us to the emergency room to talk with me further about what to expect from the hospital staff as they processed a rape kit. "Celeste, I know things are really scary right now and you probably don't trust any of us at this point, but the hospital staff is here to help you. They will take samples from inside and around your private area. We need to collect this information so we can catch the men who did this to you. Do you understand what I'm saying," she asked as she looked at my mom for her consent. All I could muster up was a nod. I couldn't even speak. I desperately wanted this to be over. "Okay. I'll need to take some photographs of the bruises on your thighs and legs as well okay," the officer whispered as she reached into her bag for her camera. I nodded again. The entire time they were performing their tests, tasks, and snapping their pictures- my eyes were shut tightly. I had hoped I could shut out this entire night, but I wasn't successful at all.

Even now as I remember that night, I'm still overwhelmed with the pain. Somehow the pain had managed to find a new home nestled away in my heart. I've tried several things to help cope with it, but to no avail. For a moment there, having a man sleep next to me seemed to help. Sex also helped to dispel the horrible memories from that night as well, for a moment. The mere thought of that night made me want to cut again. I always kept a razor in my drawer, next to my bed. I leaned over and reached in and pulled out my pink bag where my razors were kept. As I sat up against the headboard with the razor resting gently on my skin, I couldn't bring myself to do it. I wanted so badly to release the sadness, depression, and anxiety but I knew the satisfaction would only be short lived. There had to be a better way. It took everything in me not to pick up the phone and call one of my boyfriends over. But then they would want to stay, and after I got what I wanted, I'd want them to leave. Besides, the release I received from sex hadn't been satisfying me anymore. It too had become short lived and ineffective.

After fiddling around in my purse for a piece of gum, I stumbled across Mrs. Goodwin's cell phone number. She did tell me to call her anytime I wanted to talk. God knows I needed to talk to someone right now. I picked up my phone and dialed her number. Right as I was getting ready to hang up, she answered. "Hello," Mrs. Goodwin replied on the other end. I stalled for a moment, still considering hanging up. "Hi Mrs. Goodwin. This is Celeste," I whispered like a child who had just gotten herself into some trouble. "Hey baby. I was wondering when you were going to call me. I thought I was going to have to call you" she stated giggling between sentences. "So how are you sweetie," she asked as if she already knew the answer. Everything in me wanted to lie and say life was grand, but there was no way I could bring myself to do that. That's how I always answered and besides, Mrs. Goodwin had this magical way of telling when us girls were fibbing. She would look us in our eyes and say, "So which one of you is going to tell the 'real' truth?" Somehow her ability to see within my soul offered me no solace. Somehow she would still know I was lying to her.

So I took a deep breath and proceeded to tell her what really was going on with me. I told her about the rape. I told her about the men. I told her about the cutting. I could not bring myself to tell her that I was sleeping with another woman's husband though. I just couldn't. She gave me some advice and before ending our phone call, Mrs. Goodwin did what she always had done in times like these- she prayed with me. While what she said and prayed comforted me for a while, I still found my mind consumed with cutting.

Today was one of the longest and hardest days of my life, but I got through it. Before taking a hot bath and getting ready for bed, I decided to do something I hadn't done in years. Talking with Mrs. Goodwin had sparked something in me that I'd forgotten was there. I slid off the bed and onto my knees and I began to pour out my heart before God. It was like He was right there with me saying, "Celeste I see you and I hear you. I haven't abandoned or deserted you. I am here waiting for you to come back to me. I want to help you." I can't explain the peace I felt when I stood to go run my bath. I hadn't felt this way since... well, since my Sunday school classes when I was a child. I wanted more than anything to do right and be right- not just before people, but more importantly before God.

~9~
"Lead or Be Led"
(Out of the Mouth of Ms. Tangie)

I wasn't sure what it was, but it seemed to be taking me longer to get home today than any other time. The ride from Liz's house to mine, on a normal day, was about a fifteen to twenty minute ride but I swear this time it was taking me twice as long to get home. What was the problem, I thought to myself. I had my jazz music playing softly, my bottle of cranberry juice sitting next to me in the cup holder, and the top of my convertible was down so I could feel the sun on my shoulders. Maybe the ride home seemed longer because I hadn't been home in a few days and I was extremely tired and beat from this past week's events with the girls. I felt like I was involved in a boxing match- my muscles were sore, and my brain hurt. Interestingly enough, my fatigue had nothing to do with the emotional stress surrounding Richard's death and funeral, nor did it have anything to do with the chores around the house I helped Liz complete. But it had everything to do with the trauma and drama we were all dealing with in our individual lives.

"Who could this possibly be calling me," I whispered to myself while reaching down to grab my cell phone. "Hello," I answered hoping and praying this call wasn't another fire I had to put out. This firefighter was tapped and I couldn't handle anymore distress calls. "Hey Tangie," responded the voice on the other end. I paused for a moment before speaking. "Hi William," I managed to force out with a hint of sarcasm present in my voice. If William only knew how I really felt about him. Of course he'd never be able to detect it by my voice, but I was excited to hear from him. "I'm just calling to check on you. I knew you were probably on your way back home and I wanted to make sure you were okay and to let you know I was thinking about you." "Well thanks William. I am on my way home and I'm absolutely wonderful," I answered with yet more sarcasm. "Okay Tangie, I know it's not your thing to talk on the phone while driving, so I'll let you go. I'll call you a little later tonight, okay," he said as he paused and waited for a response. I was always really quick at the mouth and usually before I could finish thinking a thought, I had already blurted it out. I promised I would give myself a few moments to think before speaking and right at this very moment, I was being tested. I really didn't feel like answering him at all. I simply wanted to hang up the phone, but I was trying to better myself by working on my attitude. "Alright, William! Thanks again for calling and I'll talk with you later," I said gripping the steering wheel tightly, while rolling my eyes before hanging up. Aside from Brandon in high school, William was the only other man I had ever truly loved. There was so much inner turmoil over this entire situation though. In my heart I desperately wanted William in my life again, but in order to save face I had to cut him loose. There was something about that man that always seemed to get my blood to boiling. I was very angry and bitter at him because I felt his lack of authority in our house was part of the reason our marriage had failed, but I also loved him dearly. He had no excuse for not taking the lead, because I always paved the way for him by telling him what he needed to do. He didn't even have to think because I thought for him. Maybe that was the problem. Being told what to do definitely worked for my dad, and that would explain how I ended up with a man just like my daddy- a man I would later begin to despise.

William and I had come from similar backgrounds, but those similarities were the reasons our marriage failed in the first place. You see both William and I came from families where our mother's were the dominant figures in the house. William's mom was forced to take control and be in charge because she was a single parent and his dad was nowhere to be found. I, on the other hand, had come from a home where both parents were present- but my mom was the aggressor and my dad was the passive one. Whatever mom wanted done is exactly what got done and no one questioned her. The very fact that they remained married for as long as they did had to be proof that they possessed what it took to make marriage work, right? No matter how much I tried to convince myself our marriage would work if we followed my parent's example, I somehow knew something wasn't right about their marriage and William and I were missing something in ours.

From the very beginning, our relationship was twisted. I wanted to lead and William wanted me to lead. Everything was fine there for a moment, but then my shoulders started to get tired from carrying the load. I mentioned it several times to William, but he never responded nor did he ever step up and take his rightful place. Now I realize it wasn't that he didn't want to respond, but rather he didn't know how to respond or what to do in response to my concerns and complaints. It's amazing how, after the relationship was over, I realized my hand or my part in it ending in the first place- but I'm too far out there now to admit my wrong. I'd finally accomplished my main goal in life- I branched out and opened my own marketing firm. My problem with William came into play because I didn't trust him with handling the financial side of my business. So I stopped complaining about the "load" I had been carrying and I bared it with a fake grin, in complete silence. I didn't share how I felt about William and our marriage with anyone, not even my closest friends. I found it odd that I could be so close to them, especially Liz, and still manage to keep secrets from them. Surely this was the case with all close relationships, wasn't it? You never really tell everything.

William wanted children after the second year of our marriage, but my career had started to take off and by no means was I willing to put everything I'd worked so hard for on the back burner. Even though I promised him every year we would start a family, I knew deep down inside it would never happen. Besides, we barely knew each other and bringing a child into the picture would only complicate matters more. I'd even talked myself into trying to be submissive towards William, but it proved to be extremely hard, almost impossible. How could I possibly submit to someone who had no vision and no plan for himself, much less our marriage? The moment I opened my own marketing firm… well I knew I would never have kids, but I had no plans of telling William of my decision. I continued to take my birth control pills secretly and William assumed the timing wasn't right and that's why I never got pregnant. My persuasiveness, or manipulation as others put it, had a lot to do with William being so accepting of me not getting pregnant as well. I had become the queen of convincing others to see things from my perspective and in the process they lost sight of their own perspective. So, even though William wanted children initially, he quickly let his dream die and grabbed hold of my dream for our family and he, unknowingly, accepted my plan to never have children.

Most people, looking in at our marriage from the outside, would think we had the perfect marriage. We were financially stable and we looked good together. But, there was always something nagging at me from early on in our marriage. I knew exactly what it was, but I would never part my lips to say it. Secretly, I wanted William to take the lead, but the façade I had lived all my life prevented me from telling him so. I needed a man, my man, to tell me what we as a couple would do and when we would do it. I never had that type of relationship with a man before, not even with my father. I handled all the financial affairs in our house and William was perfectly okay with that. I made all the major decisions in the house and William was okay with that. There were times I didn't want to handle the affairs of the home and I wanted him to, but for whatever reason- he wouldn't and he didn't.

As time went on, I continued to do my thing and excelled in the corporate world and my marketing firm became very successful in the process. The money was consistently coming in and I had become a little more possessive over what I considered my money. Instead of it being our business and our money, I started viewing it as my business and my money. It was my company! My sweat, blood, and tears built it and William had nothing to do with that. Because of my impossible and stubborn mindset, my conversations with William always ended with a reminder of how much more money I made than him. I also reminded him he could leave if he didn't like the way I was handling things. William having to hear how much more successful I was over him, coupled with him finding birth control pills in my purse was too much for him to handle, so he left. I would never tell him, but I cried the entire night after he left. I didn't realize how much I missed him until he was gone. I guess the saying was true, "You never miss your water until your well runs dry." I now knew, first hand, what was meant by the saying, "Loneliness is far worse than being alone." Being alone had a lot to do with the environment and those around, but loneliness was a state of the soul. Loneliness was far worse because, at any given time, I could be surrounded by lots of people and yet I still couldn't get away from loneliness. Even though I drove William away, I longed for his companionship but I would never say so to him. I never told my girlfriends what really happened between us. I told them I couldn't take William and his ways anymore and I asked him to leave. I would never be able to live it down if they knew the truth about what really happened between William and I.

So, I led them to believe our separation and later our divorce was all my idea and very much a part of my plan. In the beginning of our marriage, getting my way was awesome. But after William left, I realized him being in my life was very much an important part of it. He brought balance, and maintaining control didn't seem all that important to me anymore. Of course I would never say that to William, so here I am today- silently enduring self-inflicted suffering. Even though my husband pleads with me to come back to him, I can't bring myself to do so nor can I admit my wrong in the whole matter. Everything in me wants him back, but I don't know how to trust him with my heart. I want to relinquish control and this false sense of security I've established, but I find it hard to believe William will be there to catch me if I let go of the control and security I've established. Even if I could go back, where would I begin? Can I even allow my heart to guide me while ridding my mind of all the control I've operated in for as long as I can remember? I don't know if it's even possible.

Often William would accuse me of not having a romantic bone in my body, but actually I was very romantic and fantasized often about us. The timing was never right with me because I always allowed my business mindset to lead and run the show. William was always a very handsome man and I fantasized often about him, but I couldn't bring myself to become free for anyone, not even my husband. I couldn't even break free from myself. I'd always operated with self-serving principles and that mindset never made allowance for me to really deal with self. I had formulated a façade that had convinced so many others and in the process, I completely lost who I was. I knew exactly when it started though. I noticed my heart becoming a little hardened towards boys and eventually men when I found out Brandon kissed and later slept with Celeste when we were teenagers. Oh sure I was angry with her and that's partly why there's always friction between us. I made myself a promise after that though. I promised I would never allow any man to get close enough to my heart to break it again. When I felt them getting too close, I'd throw up a wall to keep them out. So, not only did my self-constructed fort keep everyone else out, but it also kept me alone inside.

I never told Liz, but I was always a little jealous of her marriage. She and Richard were the perfect couple and they got along so well. I remember a conversation I had with her where she mentioned there was something she really wanted to pursue, but Richard told her he thought she should wait. My response to her was, "Girl, why do you allow that man to tell you what you can and can't do. You are crazy! Liz, I'm sure you've heard of Women's Lib. You need to check him on that girl." Liz's response was mind blowing to me. She said, "Tangie I believe Richard has my best interest at heart and I don't believe he would ever do anything to discredit, dishonor, or disrespect me. I know for a fact Richard loves me and I trust his decision for our marriage." I remember thinking how crazy Liz was to let a man dictate what she did and did not do. She obviously had been brain washed. Based on her response, I knew who ran things in their house- Richard did.

I later realized part of the problem I had wasn't solely centered on William, but more so around me and what I'd experienced. I had become a "shoe filler." No matter what problem, issue, or shoes others had placed before me, I did my very best to fix, handle, and fill them- even at the cost of my sanity. I had the awesome ability to help others fix their problems, but when it came to my issues, my problems, and my marriage- I was miserably ineffective and I constantly failed. Do you know how frustrating and maddening it is to see others experience victory and triumph in their lives while your life is steadily spiraling out of control? How is it that I could have so much insight into everyone else's life but no insight for my own?

Finally, I made it home. "Whew, what a ride," I whispered to myself as I pulled into the driveway. Here I was the owner of a very successful marketing firm with this huge house at the end of the street and no one to share it with. I could feel my life slowly spiraling out of control. I had no one else to be angry at but myself because I did this! I promised myself if William called again, I would definitely do my best to be cordial because I really did want to see him tonight. After entering the house, I realized how utterly silent it was in comparison to Liz's house when we were all there. The familiar feeling had started to set in again. No matter where I went and what I did, loneliness had a sure fire way of finding me and tonight loneliness was once again my unwanted house guest. Tonight would end just like all the others since the divorce- a hot bath, my favorite blanket, and a good book.

~10~
"You Are Hereby Summoned"

Four months had passed since I last saw my girlfriends and I was starting to really miss them. Yeah, we talked on the phone often, but I missed them nonetheless. After Tangie, Celeste, and Cat left I had time to reflect on my life and even more specifically- my life without Richard. I remember wondering how I would ever survive after his death. If the truth be told, I didn't want to live another day without him. Mrs. Goodwin was God sent though, and I'm so glad I reconnected with her. She has been a tremendous help to me in my down and "almost" out moments. Considering my mother and father are deceased and now Richard is gone, I had no one else to truly confide in but her. Mrs. Goodwin managed to talk some sense into me and she reminded me why God had me here on this earth in the first place and it wasn't solely for Richard.

It's obvious from their last visit my three girlfriends and I are all very close, but we have some unspoken truths and secrets amongst us. For whatever reason, we don't feel we can trust one another with those secrets. But I bet if most people were honest about their communication with their friends, they would also admit not having told their friends all their deep, dark secrets either. The very last thing I wanted to do was share my horrible secret. For one, I was embarrassed by it and I didn't want to open up that box of hurt again. My secret was supposed to go with me to the grave. I had never even shared it with Richard because I thought enough damage was done because I couldn't have children, but having to inform him of why I couldn't, would've been unbearable. I didn't think he could've or would've been able to handle any more devastating information, so I chose to keep it as my secret and I did everything possible to keep from sharing it. I wanted Celeste to stop with her ranting and raving that night, but she kept pushing all the right buttons and before I realized what I was saying, I had blurted out the very secret I'd managed to keep hidden all of this time.

Now here it was months later and I am faced with a new situation and yet again I've kept another secret from my friends. But, unlike the last one, I'd planned on sharing this one with them when the time permitted. Thank God He had provided me an ear and a shoulder through Mrs. Goodwin, who taught me how to better cope this time around. I will never forget how I felt when Dr. Larson came into the exam room with the results of my blood work at my last doctor's appointment. Nothing and no one could've ever prepared me for what I was about to hear. Dr. Larson's findings were very hard for me to swallow for several reasons. I sat there for a bit longer after the doctor had left so I could get myself together. This was something I knew I couldn't handle alone, so I picked up the phone and called the one person I knew would be able to give me some words of encouragement and help me regain my composure- Mrs. Goodwin. Thank God she answered. I thought it best not to tell my girlfriends, but I'd planned to share it with them at the mini reunion Mrs. Goodwin and I had been planning.

At times I sit and think, "If only Richard were here. He would know exactly what to do in a time like this." He would tell me how to handle this situation, but that's not the case anymore and now I have to figure this thing out on my own. Hopefully the girl's schedules would permit and they'd be able to attend the reunion. I guess now was as good a time as ever to call them.

"Hi Tangie. How is my big sister doing this morning," I asked with hopes all was well with her. "I'm okay Liz. How have you been," she asked with genuine concern in her voice. "Believe it or not, I am actually doing okay," I whispered realizing for the first time since Richard's death, I was actually okay. "I'm calling to invite you to a mini reunion Mrs. Goodwin and I have been planning for the last few weeks. It'll be next month on the weekend of the eighteenth. Hopefully, you're free and you can come," I shared as I waited for a response. "I am totally free that weekend and you know there is nothing that would prevent me from spending a weekend with my girls. I'll see you on the eighteenth," Tangie said excitedly. "That's awesome Tangie. I'll see you then. Love you," I whispered before hanging up. One down two more to go, I thought to myself as I picked up the phone again to call Cat.

"Hey Chris, is Cat home," I asked with a huge frown on my face. I wasn't too fond of Chris, but I respected him because he was married to one of my best friends. "Yeah Liz she's here. Hold on for a moment. Cat, Liz is on the phone," he yelled while sitting the phone down. "Hello. This is Cat," she answered obviously out of breath. "Girl what are you doing? Why are you breathing so hard," I asked curiously- really wanting to know what she was doing. "Oh, girl I was on the treadmill. What's up with you? Everything okay," she asked with a little concern in her voice. "Yeah Cat, all is well. I wanted to tell you about a mini reunion Mrs. Goodwin and I have planned for the weekend of the eighteenth. Hopefully you can come." "I don't think it'll be a problem, but let me check with my mother to see if she can watch the kids. You remember what happened with the kids the last time I came to Charlotte," she mentioned with still a remnant of anger in her voice. "Okay, check with your mom and let me know." "Alright, I will but I really don't think it will be a problem. Just put me down to come and I will work out the details with mom on tomorrow. I can't wait to see you guys again," she said excited about the reunion. "Great! Go back to Thomas the treadmill. I'll talk with you soon," I said laughingly. "You know I am girl. Love you Liz," she managed to squeeze out before saying goodbye and hanging up. I sure hope Celeste is in a good mood when I call, I thought to myself before picking up the phone.

"Hey Celeste. What have you been up to girl," I asked trying to keep the conversation light. Ever since her last visit, it had become a little hard to approach Celeste. I never knew what mood she was in- angry, depressed, or happy. So I decided to tread softly with this phone call. "Mrs. Goodwin and I have been planning a mini reunion on the eighteenth and I wanted to see if you would be able to make it," I questioned not sure which mood she would respond in. "Is that Tangie girl coming," she asked sarcastically. "Now Celeste you know Tangie will be there. This has never stopped you from coming to our gatherings before," I responded sharply but lovingly. "Yeah Liz, I'll be there. I think this time I'm going to keep my thoughts and comments to myself." "Well Celeste that's not required nor is it necessary, but if it works best for you- then by all means do just that. I want you to be just who you are- Celeste. You don't have to put on a façade for us. We are your girls and we love you. You got it," I stated bluntly. "I hear you Liz. You know I love you too girlie," she whispered as we ended our call. Now that all my girls and Mrs. Goodwin would be there, I thought this would be the perfect time to share the news I'd been living with for the last few months. Yeah, this would be the perfect time to come clean. My friendship with each of them meant way too much to me to keep this from them. Sharing was definitely in my plans for the reunion.

Later that night I sat and thought about the events that were to take place in a few weeks at the reunion, and I became a little overwhelmed and nervous about sharing what I'd managed to keep a secret. No one, and I mean absolutely no one, knew about it but me and my doctor. I hadn't even given Mrs. Goodwin the details surrounding the doctor's findings. I remember that morning four months ago like it had happened yesterday. I felt like I had been waiting on the results of my blood work for hours. I had become anxious because I wanted to know what had been causing my sickness for the past few weeks. Originally I thought it had to do with my emotions being in an uproar due to Richard's death, but as time went on, I started to feel like it was something more. I dealt with the exact same thing when mom died, but this time they seemed to hang around longer and were more intense. When I looked down at my watch, I realized I'd only been waiting for a few minutes. It seemed much longer than that though. Finally, there was a knock at the door and then entered Dr. Larson.

She pulled the rolling chair from under the desk and sat in front of me. "Well Elizabeth, the results are back from all your tests and I must tell you, I myself was not prepared for the results I found. Now I want you to take what I'm sharing with you slowly and I need you to take deep breaths," she whispered as she leaned forward towards me. As she shared her findings with me, all I could think of was, "Why God," I whispered confused and angry. Never in a million years would I expect this to happen to me at a time like this. Nonetheless, I decided I would deal with this thing head on and by no means did I plan on doing it alone. I didn't have to deal with it alone because I wasn't alone- I had my three girlfriends and the best mentor that had ever graced the face of this earth, Mrs. Goodwin. So, together with their help, I would face this thing and be victorious.

As time went on and the night before the event quickly arrived, I found myself becoming even more anxious. Not only was I excited, but I was also very nervous about how they would receive my news. Cat and Celeste were flying in on tomorrow morning and Tangie would be driving in around lunch time, but I was excited about seeing them nonetheless. Mrs. Goodwin had come into town on last night to help me get things in order around the house. She was a tremendous help.

During our reunion, it was my prayer that we would hash out any idiosyncrasies we had amongst ourselves. Sure our friendship stood the test of time, but not without its hiccups and obstacles. Hopefully, we would all come together and put our differences aside and accept one another-inadequacies and all. I really felt, for the most part, Cat and I would be able to accomplish this, but I didn't think it would be remotely possible between Celeste and Tangie though. Their differences ran deep and went way back into our childhood and I didn't think either of them was willing to swallow their pride and take the high road on the matter. But I would remain hopeful though.

As the evening wrapped up, I decided to wind down by listening to one of Richard's favorite CD's, Frankie Beverly and Maze. I hadn't listened to it since he passed away. It was way too painful to hear it before, but now I'd become a bit stronger and it didn't sting quite as much. This was due in part to me deciding to focus on all the good things Richard and I shared and dwelling on the fond memories we had as opposed to his sudden death. He was truly the ultimate husband and while I missed him tremendously, I praised God for the life He allowed me to have with Richard. As I sat there with my head resting on the back of the sofa while the soft and sensual sounds made waves throughout the room, I was truly thankful. Mrs. Goodwin had fixed us dinner earlier and she retired to her room and so I decided to spend the remainder of the evening determining what type of entertainment we'd have during the reunion. It wouldn't take much to entertain us because we've known each other almost all our lives and entertaining one another is what we did on a regular basis.

The biscuits and gravy Mrs. Goodwin made, coupled with it being well after midnight, I found myself yawning and getting sleepier by the moment. I guess it was time for me to retire. I began to climb the staircase and the memory of Richard escorting me upstairs to our bedroom the evening of our fifth wedding anniversary flooded my mind. I swear it felt like it was that night all over again. I could smell his cologne and I could even feel his touch. After snuggling under the sheets and getting comfy, I was positive I felt Richard's body heat. It was like he was sleeping right next to me with his arms around me as he had done every night. That cold, unoccupied feeling I'd felt every night since his death was not present on tonight and even though this awesome feeling was short lived, I was so very thankful for it. That warm feeling was all too familiar and all too missed and I willingly welcomed it. Even though Richard wasn't there in person, his memory lived on in me.

~11~
"All Present and Accounted For"

Morning finally arrived and I was super excited about what the day held for me and the girls. Cat phoned when she landed and I tried to pick her up from the airport, but she wouldn't let me. "Girl, I'm catching a cab right now. You've done enough planning this reunion. The least I can do is catch a cab to your house. It's not like I ain't used to it," she said as she hurried off the phone because the cab driver was blowing the horn. Celeste had also called as she was boarding her plane at BWI Airport. I was surprised because she actually sounded excited about the gathering. Tangie mentioned on last night she would be a little late because she had a few business meetings this morning and she'd be leaving right after that. Lunch had already been prepared and placed in the fridge and the house had been cleaned from top to bottom, thanks to the help of Mrs. Goodwin of course.

"Ding, dong," the doorbell sounded as I hurried towards the door while yelling to Mrs. Goodwin, "I got it!" I was not prepared for the sight on the other side of the door. Cat looked amazingly refreshed and vibrant! "Girl you look good! What have you been doing since I last saw you," I questioned jokingly but seriously. "Just taking care of myself and putting me first for a change. That's all," she confidently stated as she reached to embrace me. "The question is, what have you been doing since I was last here," Cat said as she twirled me around in a circle. "I see somebody has gotten her appetite back and she is looking good." Cat was referring to the weight I had gained since she last saw me. My appetite had come back and with a vengeance I might add. I had to pace myself where eating was concerned, because I didn't want to gain too much weight too fast. "I feel great Cat. Come on in," I said as I reached for her suitcase. As she entered the living room, Mrs. Goodwin had just come out of the kitchen and the two of them embraced and said their hellos. We all sat around the living room reminiscing on our childhood and

144

the things Mrs. Goodwin taught us as children. "You remember the time Mrs. Goodwin made you write on the board one hundred times 'I will not talk back to my Sunday school teacher'", I asked Cat as the three of us fell backwards in our chairs laughing. "Girl, do I? By the time I was done writing, the twins Arthritis and his brother Bursitis had set in." Mrs. Goodwin sat their snickering and doing her absolute best not to burst into tears from laughing so hard. "If I were to be totally honest, I would have to admit you girls gave me a run for my money. There were times when I didn't know what I would do with the four of you. God definitely had jokes where you girls were concerned." As we sat there reminiscing, I realized how much we highly esteemed Mrs. Goodwin and how valuable and lasting her lessons were to all of us, not just as kids but even now as women.

"Ding, dong." There was the doorbell again. It could only be Celeste, because Tangie hadn't finished her meetings yet. Sure enough, it was Celeste and once again she was overdressed. I still hadn't figured out, from her last visit, what was going on with her and those heavy clothes and heavy makeup she wore. Now here she was again looking the exact same way. I was extremely happy to see her nonetheless. "Hey girl," I shouted as we hugged. Before I could announce her arrival, Cat and Mrs. Goodwin had already made their way to the foyer. "Hey Celeste," Cat whispered as she reached out and hugged her with what was obviously a heartfelt embrace. Celeste stood frozen and confused at the sincerity of Cat's embrace. Mrs. Goodwin also embraced her and whispered, "It's so good to see you again." The two of them kept in touch after the last visit and I thought that was awesome- just what Celeste needed. Celeste had someone to confide in and that did my heart good.

We all headed into the living room where we, once again, sat around reminiscing about our childhood. "Celeste we were just talking about the time Mrs. Goodwin made Cat write one hundred times on the board." "Oh yeah, that was hilarious. Every five minutes, Cat would turn around and look at us with the sad face and we would burst out into laughter," shouted Celeste as she slapped her knees with excitement. It was good seeing her smiling again. I'd forgotten how beautiful her smile was because we hardly ever saw it anymore. This reunion was already off to a great start and prayerfully it would end even better.

About an hour later, there was a knock at the door. Surely it wasn't Tangie because she always rang the doorbell. Oh but it was her and with an armful of gifts. She couldn't ring the bell because her arms were full. "Oh girl, let me help you with those," I said as I reached to take two gifts from her right hand. She'd brought gifts for all of us, including Celeste. Wow! What was the world coming to? After managing to make it into the house, Tangie sat in the first available chair while attempting to catch her breath. "Whew. Those steps are a killer Liz, especially when you're loaded down with gifts," Tangie said laughingly while we all fiddled through the gifts trying to find the one with our names on it. "Dang, Santa! What's the occasion," Cat asked jokingly as she continued to look for a gift with her name on it. "And why must I have an occasion Ms. Cat," Tangie asked as she

147

smiled. "I really wanted you guys to know how much I love and appreciate you being in my life, that's all. You know I'm not one for voicing how I feel, but I am the bomb at buying gifts that demonstrate such," Tangie mentioned as she pointed towards the packages she brought in with her.

Just as we were all settling down to open our gifts, Mrs. Goodwin stepped into the kitchen. It had finally started to resonate with me just how much I loved these ladies. Where would I be and who would I be without them experiencing every inch of this life with me. Mrs. Goodwin returned with colorful envelopes in her hand and each of our names was written on one. What was she up to? She hadn't mentioned anything to me about us playing any games during the reunion. Come to think of it though, Mrs. Goodwin was always full of surprises. Well, I guess I'd have to wait right along with the others to see what she had planned for us this evening.

After sitting and talking for what seemed like hours, we began winding down and snuggling even further into our chairs. Mrs. Goodwin picked up the colorful envelopes on the table beside her and handed each of us the one with our name on it. But before we were allowed to open them, Mrs. Goodwin spoke. "Ladies, true friendship is only as strong as the "true glue" or the trust that binds it together. In every meaningful relationship, honesty and transparency are required if it will ever stand the test of time. You ladies have been friends for over twenty years and I believe trust is what has held you together for this length of time. But just as glue loses its potency, power, and grip over time- so does relationships where the trust has not been reinforced. So, with that being said, each of you will be given an opportunity to open your envelope and read aloud the words of wisdom I wrote for you. When you are done reading, you will then have the opportunity to be transparent and honest with one another by participating in confession time- if you choose to. You can share as much or as little as you want, but keep in mind the more you open up, the more the others will open up. The choice is yours though. Understood ladies," Mrs. Goodwin asked as she panned the room to see if there were any objections. There were none.

"Well I guess I'll go first", Cat whispered. I'm a little nervous, but willing to share nonetheless. Words of wisdom, let's see," she whispered as she pulled the card from the envelope and read it aloud. "Overriding the truth and what we know to be right temporarily fills the gaps and voids we experience. Shortly thereafter, those gaps and voids become larger, deeper, and even harder to climb out of. Sometimes the very things we want and desire the most are indeed the exact opposite of what it is we really need. The grass is not greener on the other side! Closer observation quickly reveals you're simply looking at a mirage- one your heart and mind has fabricated to satisfy the overwhelming desires you, yourself, instituted and developed. In fact, the more you chase after the mirage, the thirstier you'll become and satisfaction will forever remain a dream," Cat read as she placed the card in her lap and folded her hands as a somber look completely enveloped her. She looked like a child who had just been told she wouldn't be getting the new bike she'd been hoping for on Christmas. You know- that look of utter disappointment. "Wow! Okay Mrs. Goodwin. After having read those words, they've caused me to feel, I don't know... sad, hurt, and angry. As hard as it was reading what you wrote, I somehow feel the hardest part I have yet to experience. It feels like I'm being ripped apart- like a part of me died just from reading your note," Cat whispered as she prepared herself for the confession she was about to reveal to us. It was obvious this was very uncomfortable for her, because she kept brushing imaginary dust balls from her lap. "Well girls, you may have realized Chris and I haven't been doing too well in our marriage. It's been really hard trying to adjust in a marriage where love is obviously not present anymore. Our marriage is now a marriage of convenience- one where our children have become the glue that keeps us together. In the beginning, I needed Chris and he needed me- almost like a business transaction. Rather than lovers, we've become more like roommates who occasionally engage in conjugal visits," she said looking a little embarrassed. "Have you ever had one of those moments of clarity in life where you knew the right thing to do, but it wasn't necessarily the easiest thing to do? You know the moment when what everyone expects of you is the easiest thing to do even though it goes against everything you hold dear? Well prior to marrying Chris, I had one of those moments of clarity, but I chose to marry him despite what my heart and head were saying. Besides, that's what everyone expected of me- the nice, wholesome, church-going girl. I guess what I'm trying to say is, I married Chris even though I knew I didn't love him and I knew he wasn't saved. Our different religious views, or his lack thereof, didn't help matters much either. Over the years, I tried to convince myself God would work out our marital issues and our marriage would be just fine. But the one thing I failed to take into consideration was God could do nothing apart from us wanting and allowing Him to do it- no matter how long I stayed on my knees and how hard I prayed, God saw the lack of genuineness in my heart. I felt we needed counseling, but Chris refused. He said there was nothing anyone could tell him about our marriage," Cat shared as she began to sob softly. Immediately, Mrs. Goodwin handed her a tissue and assured her she was amongst friends who loved her and wanted the very best for her. "Is there anything else you want to share Cat," Mrs. Goodwin asked softly. "Well...yeah. I can't begin to tell you how much I longed for compliments, and just the attention of my husband- hoping and praying it would be enough to make a difference in this thing we called a marriage. Chris had long since stopped paying me any attention and I longed for true companionship and just the whole consciousness of being in love. I've heard women talk about how completely in love they are and my entire being wants so badly to experience it as well. I long and thirst for this utopia that seems to have been deemed "off limits" to me, but I deserve to be in love and have it reciprocated back to me! Finally, I get a glimpse of what I think being in love looks and feels like and now I must let it go," she said as she dropped her face in her hands in despair. I know you're all probably wondering who I'm referring to. A few months ago, I ran into an old friend from college and since our encounter, we've kept in touch. Well, he asked to see me a few weeks ago and I agreed," Cat whispered as she looked up to see the expressions on our faces. "Now I can't seem to get this man out of my system. I can't begin to explain how he makes me feel. Chris isn't aware of any of this, but I know I have to tell him. I know better than anyone that my relationship with Michael is not of God, but I can't bring myself to end it," she shared ashamedly. The room was completely silent. No one knew what to say because the very last person we expected to act in this manner was Cat. She was always the cautious and careful one. "Well ladies, is there anything you want to say to Cat," Mrs. Goodwin asked as she looked around the room. "Cat, why did you feel you couldn't share this with us," Tangie asked. "I was ashamed. Ashamed because my marriage was failing and I allowed myself to fall for another man," Cat added. "Well we love you nonetheless Cat," I said before placing my arm around her and kissing her on her cheek. "Cat one of the worst forms of bondage to be involved in is people bondage.

People bondage causes you to be concerned about what others think and say above what God thinks and says about you. It takes on a form of idolatry as well because you've placed someone and their opinions over God and His expectations of you. Now concerning the other man in the picture- you must let him go! You will quickly see that what you are experiencing with him is merely a fantasy that has been borne out of the voids and neglect you've experienced from your childhood and from Chris. You've developed a soul tie with this man and now emotional strongholds have set in. Emotional strongholds are tricky in that they cause you to believe the fantasy world could actually become a successful reality, but that couldn't be further from the truth. The reality of it is you are a Christian woman who's married. If no one else holds you at a higher standard, God does. While this other man may mean well in his compliments, you are in no position to be enticed in any manner considering the shape your marriage is in. Yes it's going to be hard to cut him loose, but absolutely necessary. If you don't end the relationship now, you are only heaping more heartache into you future- making it even harder to come out from under. Remember, God never changes His mind concerning His word- no matter how much you think your specific situation warrants it. My advice to you is to take some time and seek God and give Him a chance to tell you His thoughts and plans for your life. You didn't allow God this opportunity before you got married and if you don't allow it now, you are destined to repeat your past mistakes and experience yet another void. Do you understand what I'm telling you," Mrs. Goodwin asked as she touched Cat on her knee. "Yes ma'am, I understand." "Well, who wants to go next," Mrs. Goodwin asked. No one answered, so we decided to take a short refreshment break. Mrs. Goodwin headed to the kitchen and returned with sandwiches and drinks. We all sat quietly and nervously eating like we were about to take a major test afterwards. This exercise was definitely strengthening us, but I had a strong feeling things were about to get a little more heated as the evening went on.

~12~
"How Low Can You Go?"

After we were all done eating and the small talk had ceased, Mrs. Goodwin turned to Tangie, "Well Tangie, why don't you share your words of wisdom next." Tangie reached into her envelope and began to share the words Mrs. Goodwin had written to her. "Pride never exposes itself. It never owns up to what it is. Pride destroys relationships and so much more. Tangie, just when you think you've got it all under control, pride secretly sets you up and highlights your name in bold. It puts you on blast and brings up your past. Yeah, those who possess it seem to have it all together, but God's word warns pride comes right before the fall." As Tangie read the words aloud, her voice began to soften. I couldn't figure out if it softened because she was embarrassed about what she was reading or if, for the first time, she realized pride was the name of the monster she had been dealing with most of her life. Either way, Mrs. Goodwin's words were causing a stir in her, one that we'd never seen before. "Okay. This is some heavy stuff. The more I read what you wrote, the more I realize I've dealt with this thing all my life. I would've never been honest with myself or even wise enough to peg this thing as pride because as you mentioned in the note, pride will never self-expose," she whispered as she placed the note in her lap and sat silently. Everyone was silent because it wasn't the norm for us to see Tangie express any emotions- happy, sad, or anything for that matter. This was a first for us all and we were definitely shocked by her reaction to the note. "Ladies, is there anything you want to say to Tangie," Mrs. Goodwin asked. No one had any comments. Heck, none of us knew how to respond to what we'd just witnessed! "Okay Tangie, what is it you would like to share with the ladies," Mrs. Goodwin asked sitting back in her chair as she crossed her legs and waited on a response. Tangie eventually got herself together and cleared her throat before sharing. "Alright girls, you remember when William and I separated and I told you I asked him to leave? Well, it didn't quite happen like that.

158

Whew, this is hard. Well... William left me," she said as she wiped the sweat from her brow and exhaled while dropping her head in embarrassment and shame. Tears, something none of us had ever witnessed before from her, had begun to trickle down her face. She tried everything within her power to stop them, but the flood gates had opened and the tears flowed. Cat and I attempted to console her, but Celeste didn't move an inch.

"I know I had you guys believing I was in control of my life- especially my marriage, but I'm not. I never was! William left because he couldn't take the verbal abuse and my controlling ways anymore. I thought I would be okay without him. You know... since I owned my own business and was financially stable," she stated looking around the room for approval. "I thought I didn't need him, but I couldn't have been further from the truth. I've put on a really good act, but I am absolutely miserable. Sometimes I feel as though I merely exist, and have yet begun to live life. Do you guys even know the difference between being alone and loneliness? When you're alone, you're the only one in the room and solitude is based on those things around you- your external environment. Oh, but that's not the case with loneliness. Loneliness screams from the depths of your soul and even though no one else can hear it, you can't seem to shut it up. Loneliness causes you to be surrounded by thousands of people and still experience such desolation, not even those closest to you can pull you out of. Since William left, I've dealt heavily with loneliness- to the point that I've battled depression and even had to take medication for it. The weird thing about this whole situation is that William wants me back, but my pride won't let me admit how much I want and need him. Now I know that it's pride that keeps my lips from apologizing and admitting my wrong," she whispered. "It'll be okay Tangie," I whispered as I handed her a tissue. It was hard seeing my friend hurt. I wanted more than anything to console her and take away the hurt she was feeling, but I couldn't- none of us could.

"Tangie, I would venture to say you've learned something about yourself tonight you weren't aware of. You've learned you are human-

yes, flesh and blood. You feel and experience things just as the rest of us do. You are not some emotionless robot who bleeds oil instead of blood. For whatever reason, you've convinced yourself you must always be the tough one- the one who has been given the sole responsibility of making sure everyone else is okay- even at the expense of you, yourself, not being okay. But Tangie, it is perfectly alright to say no. It is okay to admit you can't handle everyone else's problems because you have your own overwhelming issues. Pride has this awesome way of causing you to think no one else can do things quite as good as you can, so now you run yourself ragged trying to do it all. Superwoman does not exist-not now, not ever. You cannot manage your stuff and theirs too, and attempting to do such will kill you. The very façade you've put in place to convince others you're in control will fall apart at the most inopportune time. Before you realize it, you've locked yourself away in the solitary confinement of your own jail. Pride will destroy you and everything you've worked so hard for," Mrs. Goodwin added as she slid to the edge of her chair so she could look Tangie in her eyes and express the seriousness behind the matter of pride.

"Mrs. Goodwin, I don't know where to begin with this whole pride thing," Tangie whispered as she wiped her eyes. "Don't worry sweetie, you aren't alone. We got your back," she said as she pointed at each of us. We all stood as we placed our arms around her. Tangie had always been the lead in this girl group and now we were beginning to realize how all that responsibility had, in fact, hurt her and not helped her. The room was silent once again, as we all settled back into our chairs.

"Celeste, why don't you go next," Mrs. Goodwin mentioned as she headed to the kitchen to get more refreshments. When she returned, she looked over towards Celeste. "Okay sweetie. We're ready," she whispered. Celeste slowly pulled the card out of her envelope and proceeded to read it. "It is very possible to experience freedom from guilt after abuse. What happened to you was not your fault! The journey to freedom and healing is only found in bringing your lonely, wounded heart- full of rage and hurt, overwhelmed with doubt- before

God. Celeste, God promised He wouldn't brush aside the bruised and the hurt and He wouldn't disregard the small and insignificant, but He would steadily and firmly set things right. Sometimes healing will only come through facing the very thing that has caused the hurt in the first place. Even before a car can travel in the right direction, it must first back up and turn around," she read aloud as she did everything within her power to push back the tears that had begun to well up in her eyes while reading the note. Somehow we knew we had yet to see the real Celeste come forth, and so we sat quietly. "You know as I read your words Mrs. Goodwin, I couldn't help but think about how I inflicted the same hurt I felt all those many years ago on those around me. The pain was imposed and forced on me as a child and I internalized and incubated it, and without realizing it, I spewed it right back out on anyone and everyone in my vicinity." We all sat there trying to anticipate what she would say next. "Ladies, do you have anything to say to Celeste," Mrs. Goodwin asked softly. None of us wanted to say anything, so we kept quiet.

"Celeste, are you ready to share your secret with the ladies?" Celeste began crying quietly even before she had begun to share. This was not a good sign. The secret she had been holding was obviously a big one. She stood gently and began to slowly roll up her left sleeve and then the right sleeve. Based on the looks on all our faces, none of us had any idea what she was up to. She made her way to the middle of the floor, as she slowly turned her arms outward-revealing what looked liked alligator skin. Her arms were covered in hundreds of cuts and whelps that had healed, but looked and felt like leather. "Oh my God Celeste, what have you done," I asked while pushing back the tears that had begun to burn in their ducts. Celeste stood sobbing and obviously ashamed of what she'd just revealed. "I've cut every day since the age of eighteen, with the exception of the week I spent with you guys a few months ago," she whispered softly as the tears continued to trickle down her cheeks and onto her blouse. We were all dumbfounded by this time. We didn't know what to think or say to her. How could this have happened right under our noses? As close as we were to her, we were totally ignorant to what she was dealing with. Were we that caught up in our own lives that we didn't recognize Celeste's obvious screams for help? "I know you're all asking how I could've done this to myself or how could I have deliberately hurt myself? Well, if you've dealt with the nightmares, heartaches, and inner turmoil I've been dealing with over the years- you would completely understand. In the beginning, the only way I would feel relief from what was taunting me was to cut myself. After a while cutting was no longer effective, so I introduced sex into the process," she said visibly embarrassed at what had become of her life. We all stood to embrace her empathetically. Even Tangie let go of her issues with Celeste and genuinely embraced her for the first time in years. "It is in this environment that your relationships are fortified and reinforced. Ladies, there's nothing the four of you will ever be faced with or come up against that you can't overcome with the help of one another. True friendship is rare and precious, but you've proven it's definitely possible," Mrs. Goodwin whispered as she sat back in her chair admiring the four of us standing there.

Once we were all seated, eyes dried, and breathing regulated- Celeste mentioned she had another secret she needed to share. "This secret has been eating at the very core of me for years. I believe it, along with the assault, has contributed to and perpetuated my cutting. No matter how I try to run from this, I can't! Have you ever been involved with something or someone you knew you should not have been involved with? You know that person or thing that was totally off limits? Remember when you guys asked who the "mystery man" was? Liz, I believe you referred to him as being the one constant thing in my life," she said as she turned to look at me for agreement. "Yeah, I remember Celeste. So, who is he," I asked not sure if I even wanted to know the answer. Celeste turned back around and faced Cat. "Cat, I'm so sorry," Celeste muttered as she began to cry again. "What exactly are you sorry about Celeste," Cat asked confused. "I didn't mean for it to happen- it just did. I've been seeing Chris for the past six years," Celeste said flinching as she closed her eyes to block out the looks. We all quickly looked at Cat for a response. Cat sat there for a moment, with her mouth hung open as she began to cry. Hurt and anger were soon present on her face and before we knew what happened, Cat lunged from her seat and tackled Celeste while screaming, "How could you Celeste! How could you!" Tangie and Mrs. Goodwin bolted from their seats and did everything in their power to pull Cat off of Celeste. Celeste had done the unthinkable, the lowest of the low amongst friends.

Cat stormed out of the room extremely upset. Mrs. Goodwin followed after her. Celeste sat on the couch, ashamed of what she had done to Cat- to all of us. "Celeste, what were you thinking? You know what, don't even answer that. You weren't thinking," Tangie spewed out angrily at her. I sat there in my chair still in shock. How could someone you viewed closer than a sister do something so terrible? Pity is what I felt for Celeste as I sat and watched her. Eventually, Mrs. Goodwin returned to the room and Cat followed behind her shortly thereafter. Cat refused to come back into the living room though. She sat at the kitchen table where she could still hear the conversation. She couldn't bear to look at Celeste again without wanting to kill her and I couldn't blame her either. "From this point on, Cat has agreed to listen to the remainder of the session. She chooses not to say anything else," Mrs. Goodwin whispered as she looked over at Celeste. "Celeste, why would you deliberately hurt those closest to you? Did you not think about how this would turn out or how it would affect everyone involved," Mrs. Goodwin asked. Celeste was quiet for a moment, but started to speak softly. "I have no excuse Mrs. Goodwin. All I knew was that I was hurting and I needed something, or someone to stop it. It was not my intent to get involved with my best friend's husband. I was in their wedding remember," Celeste mentioned as if it would be enough to excuse her behavior. "Chris approached me at the wrong time in my life. I was down, depressed, needy, and most of all lonely and he was the pill that seemed to fix what was ailing me. Eventually, that moment turned into years and I became dependent on that "pill." I had every intention of ending the relationship, but Chris tunneled through to that vulnerable place I forgot I possessed and no one saw since the attack. He saw the cuts on my arms and that hard shell I'd encased myself in all my life, the one that kept everyone at a distance, broke in half. Now the very person I needed to rid myself of was the one person who'd managed to see me- shortcomings, inadequacies, bad habits, addictions and all- and he chose to stay," Celeste whispered softly. "I absolutely needed him in my life," she exclaimed.

I didn't know how to feel at this point. A part of me pitied Celeste and felt sorry for her, but there was also a part of me that worried about how this would affect Cat and the children. Emotionally, I was all over the place. Celeste finally quieted down as it was obvious she was done with her secrets and I was glad because I wasn't sure how many more we could handle. I knew this exercise was supposed to bring us together, but I didn't see how it would be possible between Cat and Celeste at this point. Nonetheless, I still hadn't shared my secret and hopefully it would have the adverse effect on the ladies.

"Liz, hopefully things are calm enough for you to read your card and share something with us," Mrs. Goodwin stated as we all sat back in our chairs again. I had begun to feel a little anxious so I slowly, but deeply began inhaling and exhaling to calm myself down. I pulled my card out of the envelope and began to read what Mrs. Goodwin had written. "Liz, everyone has experienced fear at some point in their lives. The intent of fear is to keep you still an immobilized so you never advance any further than where you are right now. What happens with water when it becomes stagnant? It develops mold and fungus and is no longer fit for consumption. It's no longer any good to anyone. But God has given you the necessary tools to overcome this powerful emotion called fear. Yes, Richard is no longer here with you, but you are more than capable of living a productive and happy life even now, apart from him. God, your Maker is your husband. So look now to God for His provision and protection for you. He is there waiting to fill every void you've experienced or will experience from Richard's death. Look to Him Liz! Remember, you are not in this alone. Your girlfriends are here- with open arms, open minds, and open hearts- waiting to embrace you and anything you have or will ever have to go through." Reading those words brought tears to my eyes.

I took a deep breath and looked around the room to see if anyone had anything to say. No one did, so I continued with my secret. "Well girls, I've been holding this for a few months now and it has been extremely hard keeping it from you. You all know I had a doctor's appointment on the morning you went back home after the funeral right," I asked as I looked around the room again as they all nodded and agreed. "Well the doctor laid some heavy news on me at the appointment. To put it plainly, she found a growth in my stomach," I whispered as I dropped my head in relief- relief that I had gotten it out without falling apart. "Oh my God Liz- seriously," Cat asked concerned as she made her way back to the living room. "Yeah, the doctor said it was an aggressive growth," I mentioned as I watched the hurt and sad looks cover their faces. I proceeded to stand and slowly lift my shirt to show them exactly what I was referring to. Once my stomach was visible, I rested both hands on it. I can't explain their facial expressions as they stared in awe at how large my stomach had gotten from the mass. Before I could say another word, they all began to cry. "Girls, it's okay. I'll be fine- I promise," I stated attempting to calm them down, but it was too late. "Cat, Tangie, Celeste," I yelled trying to calm them down and get their attention. "I'm not sick. I'm pregnant," I screamed while closing my eyes to try and rid myself of the looks of hurt on their faces. "You're what! How can you be pregnant Liz? You can't have any children, right," Tangie asked confused as she slowly wiped the tears from her eyes. Their facial expressions went from being overwhelmed with sadness to being consumed with shock. "According to the results from my blood tests, I'm pregnant. From what the doctor determined, I'm at least five months," I shared as I smiled while rubbing my slightly swollen belly. This news was bittersweet to me. The one desire Richard and I had was to have a baby and now I miraculously end up pregnant after his death. "So Liz, how…, I mean what happened," Cat further questioned still confused by the information I just revealed to them. "The only thing I could think of is a few weeks before Richard died, we were intimate almost every night and I must've conceived then. I guess when we finally decided to remove the self-inflicted pressure we placed on ourselves, it just happened," I whispered as I stood their admiring my baby bump.

For that brief moment, I had all my girlfriends back together in unison. We'd all lowered our defenses, buried the hatchets, and dropped our issues with one another- if only for a moment, as we bonded again and rejoiced together. This was exactly how friendship was supposed to feel- warm, close knit, and familiar. They all wanted to rub my belly and I wanted each of them to experience this moment with me. Mrs. Goodwin sat back in her chair with the biggest smile on her face. I hadn't seen her smile like that in a while. "Ladies, this is a beautiful sight- seeing all of you embracing and rejoicing with one another, as you lay your differences down- even if but for a moment. This is the behavior that reinforces the true glue or the trust I mentioned earlier," she stated as she gleamed with happiness.

It wasn't too long before Cat and Celeste were at it again. So, we ended the evening's events and everyone retired to their prospective rooms for the night. Mrs. Goodwin and I sat a little longer and talked before retiring to our bedrooms. The weekend was rapidly winding down and there was so much more I desired to share with my friends. Just before leaving for their homes the following morning, I asked each of them to join me for breakfast. "Ladies, I have something for each of you," I mentioned as I handed each of them a small box that I'd gift wrapped. "Before you open your gifts, I would like to say how happy and fortunate I am to have you all in my life. Through the thick and the thin, you all have stood by me and weathered the storms right along with me and I love you for that," I mentioned as I motioned for them to open their gifts. In each of the boxes were small photo albums that contained pictures from our childhood up until our last visit together. On the very last page of each photo album was a copy of the ultrasound picture I had performed on last week. "Oh yeah, I'm having a boy and his name is RJ- short for Richard, Jr.," I said grinning from ear to ear. "It's because of God, Mrs. Goodwin, and our Sunday school classes that we were brought together in the beginning and it is because of God, Mrs. Goodwin and this reunion that we have all been brought together again. If I haven't told you before, I love you all so very much," I whispered as the four of us embraced in a group hug. As they headed to their rooms to finish packing for their flights and drive home, Mrs. Goodwin helped me clear the table. While standing at the kitchen sink, she turned and faced me. "Liz, you know this visit was important for the longevity of your friendship? Even though some of the secrets that were revealed here on last night were earth shattering, they needed to be told nonetheless. There's something about finally sharing those deep, dark secrets that allow the bearer to now be positioned to walk in freedom- unhindered. Sure, some of the relationships may not continue in the manner in which they were prior to the secrets being exposed, but it releases the guilt of hiding it and erases any area for the enemy to bring guilt to the bearer," Mrs. Goodwin spoke softly but assuredly. No sooner than she had finished talking did I hear a horn blowing outside. It was Celeste's cab waiting to take her to the airport. Celeste made her way downstairs and sat her bags at the front door as she headed towards where I now sat in the living room. Sitting down beside me, Celeste began to speak, "Liz, I am so sorry for all the drama I brought to your home. I never intended to hurt any of you. I can only hope you can find it in your heart to forgive me and not toss me aside." "Celeste, I will always love you no matter what. But there are some things in friendships you just don't do. After seeing how what you've done has hurt Cat, and the rest of us for that matter- I now hope and pray you will seek help with this. I can't explain how much it hurts to know you battle with all this stuff and we had no clue of it. But, I will stay in touch and check in with you because more than anything, I want the Celeste I remember back- healthy and whole. I love you girl," I whispered as we embraced. I walked her to the door and watched her get into the cab. I prayed she recognized she wasn't in this fight alone, and that she knew I would always be here to help her. Somewhere, deep down inside, I knew the friendship between the four of us would never be the same again.

No sooner did Celeste leave in the cab, did another pull up out front. I waved to the driver to let him know I saw him and I turned and yelled upstairs for Cat to come down. As I watched her waggle with her bags, I could see heaviness on her shoulders. I couldn't imagine what her life would be like when she returned home. "Hey baby," I whispered as I put my arms around her. I expected her to start crying, but obviously she was all cried out- no tears fell. "You ready to get home and see those beautiful babies of yours," I asked trying to spark a normal conversation with her, but all I got was a head nod. "Well Cat, I want you to know I love you and I am right here. I can't pretend to act as if I know what you're feeling right now, because I don't- but I can say 'This too shall pass'." She looked at me with such a lifeless look in her eyes and then she squeezed my hand and that was all I needed to know that the friend I knew and loved was still in there somewhere. "I love you baby," I whispered in her ear as I embraced her again. "I love you more," she responded back before grabbing her bags and heading down the stairs and into the cab awaiting her. I had no clue as to which road her life would take now, but if I knew anything about Cat- I knew she was a fighter and nothing could keep her down.

After closing the front door, I could hear pots clanking in the kitchen. Before I could reach the door to see who it was Mrs. Goodwin exited. "Hey baby, I was just straightening up in there before I left to go back home," she mentioned as she headed over to her luggage on the floor in the dining room. "Mrs. Goodwin you've done more than enough for us. I would've gotten those dishes." "I know Liz, but I want you to relax after we're gone. You have another passenger on board," she whispered as she smiled and pointed at my belly. "Take care of yourself sweetie and please keep in touch," she spoke gently while hugging me. I watched her as she headed to her car. "There goes an awesome woman of God who has no problem telling us like it is," I thought to myself while smiling.

Tangie and her luggage finally tumbled down the stairs and into the living room where I sat on the couch flipping through a magazine. "Whew. This is one beat chic," she said as she smiled at me. "So, mommy dearest, what are you going to do when I leave," she said again smiling at me. "Well I guess the only thing to do is enjoy the peace and quiet," I mentioned smiling back at her. "Well I guess you're right on that one. You know I love you right," she asked while smiling at me. "Yes mom, you have made that perfectly clear," I spoke sarcastically. "Good and don't you ever forget it! I must say, when I found out what Mrs. Goodwin had planned with all that confession stuff, I had an internal come-apart. But, I'm glad we all participated because healing is inevitable. I can honestly say there has been a weight lifted off my shoulders and I am excited about getting back home and talking with William about us," she spoke softly as she flipped through a magazine. "I'm happy to hear that Tangie. I must confess, I was a little uneasy myself but I too am glad it happened the way it did in the environment that it did." "I love you girl and you to RJ," Tangie said as she leaned over and kissed my forehead right before rubbing my belly. "Well, I must be hitting this road and quickly. They're calling for rain and I don't want to get caught in it," she said while picking up her luggage and heading out the front door. Out of the three of my girlfriends, Tangie seemed to have benefited the most from our exercise on last night. Not only were her steps lighter, but her mindset had shifted somehow. She had begun to "feel" again. Great things were in store for her and her marriage and I couldn't wait to hear all about it. Finally, I had my house to myself again and all I wanted to do was sit back, put my feet up, and relax.

Tangie hadn't been gone for more than thirty minutes before the door bell rang. "What did that girl forget this time? She would forget her head if it wasn't attached to her body," I whispered jokingly.

As I reached the door and slowly opened it, there stood a woman on the other side and by the look on her face, she was uneasy about something. "Yes, can I help you," I asked as I stood there with my hand resting on my belly. "I'm looking for Elizabeth Frazier, do you know her," the woman whispered softly. "Well...yeah. I'm Elizabeth Frazier and who are you," I questioned. The uneasy look she possessed earlier had now turned into a warm smile as she extended her hand to greet me. I became even more confused by the minute, and not to mention very curious. Who was this stranger standing on my front porch? She began to speak again as her hand remained extended waiting for me to return the greeting. "My name is Vanessa- Vanessa Palmer. I know you don't know me, but I believe we both have something or someone in common. I'm Richard's half-sister," she whispered softly. "Richard's half-sister! But he didn't have any siblings or at least he wasn't aware of any. How did you find me," I questioned beginning to feel a little weak in the knees from the excitement of the news. "My mom mentioned, on her death bed, she'd had a son and had given him up for adoption. After she passed away, I was determined to find the only other relative I had on the face of this earth. I had to find Richard! All the legal documents I ran across pointed me towards an obituary. I wanted so desperately to believe I had been searching out the wrong Richard Frazier, but indeed I hadn't. The obituary led me to you," she whispered as her eyes became glassy with tears. After drying the tears running down my face, I eventually greeted her with a hug and a warm smile and I invited her in. "Please, please come in Vanessa." God had jokes! Not only did he leave me a mini replica of Richard in baby RJ, but He had smiled even brighter upon me and left me a sister and RJ an aunt with whom we could share the rest of our lives.

Previously I had been overwhelmed with sorrow, but the sorrow I endured paled in comparison to the new found joy I was experiencing at this very moment. There was so much to talk about and discover, but there was also no need to rush because all Vanessa, RJ, and I had was time. I now realized God had allowed me many, many moments of refreshing. Even through my darkest hour and my most heated battle, He was right there providing guidance and comfort. Yes, my girlfriends and I had many more hills to climb and valleys to cross together, but I was positive God would see us through all of that as well. I had reached a favorable conclusion over the last five months- every dark cloud had a silver lining. All we had to do was look up from where we were and grasp it. I found yet another silver lining in one of my dark clouds, and I was absolutely positive it was dusted with gold. Life, for me, was great and getting better by the moment!

Words of Wisdom...

Healthy friendships are those in which there's reciprocation- giving and receiving on both ends. Healthy friendships are never one-sided, where one person is always on the receiving end. If you find your friendship isn't one of reciprocation, by all means have a heart to heart talk. If nothing is resolved, then it is perfectly okay to "**redefine**" the relationship. The best of friendships endure ups and downs, good and bad times- but remaining strong for one another throughout the rough times is "true" friendship.

Remember: Not everyone was designed to be your friend, nor were you designed to be a friend to everyone and it is perfectly okay.

Wishing you lifelong, "true" friendships-

Pam

www.pamelaharriswilliams.com